A Chicken Was There
At Christmas

Throughout History and Around the World,
When the Sun Rose on Christmas Morning,
A Chicken Was There

A.A. Davenport

Independently Published

ISBN: 9798338129883

For Denise

Contents

Christmas Trees and Proper English Squirrels, Windsor Castle, England, 1850

My missus didn't start the crazy tradition of putting a tree in the house every year at Christmas, but it's because of my missus that having a tree indoors is popular today. Personally, I don't think trees belong indoors because of the squirrels. Squirrels are sneaky and if a squirrel was hiding in the tree when they brought it inside, it could get loose. Squirrels are very messy, and they have fleas. If a squirrel got loose in Windsor Castle, then my mister and missus could get fleas as well. The Queen of England should not be bothered by squirrel fleas. Besides, why should squirrels be allowed in the castle when chickens aren't? Chickens don't have fleas, sometimes a chicken can have mites, but everyone knows that mites are not as bad as fleas. If chickens can't come in, then squirrels shouldn't be allowed either, at least that's what I think.

The Christmas tree tradition started because my mister, Prince Albert, comes from a country called Germany, and apparently, they've been bringing trees (and probably squirrels) indoors at Christmastime for years. But it was when my missus, Queen Victoria, decided to have a Christmas tree that the whole world started to notice. My missus is very popular. A few years ago, a magazine printed a picture of my missus and mister and all the children around the Christmas tree and now everyone wants to have a Christmas tree too. Speaking of the children, why are the children allowed in the castle when the chickens aren't? Chickens are the same as children, in fact, we're a little bit better since we're a lot less trouble than children, and we lay eggs. Children don't lay eggs, at least I don't think they do.

Maybe this will be the year when everything changes and I'll be allowed to come inside the castle and enjoy the Christmas tree with the rest of the family. You see, I saved young Prince Alfred's life a couple of years ago and because of that I'm royalty now. But not just royalty, I'm in the line of succession to the throne! I'm not the heir to the throne, but I'm pretty sure I'm the spare, and this is how it happened.

Several years ago, my mister sent all the way to Germany for a spruce fir tree. The day it arrived I went out to inspect it for squirrels. I definitely didn't want German squirrels in the castle, if we were destined to have squirrels running about the Queen's bedroom, they would need to be proper English squirrels.

Since the tree was out in the gardener's shed, I took the long way around so I could stop on the lawn and get some breakfast. Though I'm not supposed to wander around the castle lawns, I do it anyway because of the fat worms that like to live in the grass. Worms are one of my favorite snacks. Besides, I've noticed that there are a lot of swans lounging on the lawn, why can't the chickens do that too? Of course we aren't lazy like swans, we don't want to just sit there preening and acting like everyone wants to look at us all the time. Swans are a bit snooty. Back to my story...

After eating a couple of worms, I decided to head around to the kitchen at the back of the castle in case they had some bits of leftover cake to share. That's where I saw them making the treats they wanted to hang on the tree. The cook had a large pot boiling over the pit and they were boiling sugar in that pot. When the sugar turned into a syrup, they poured it into molds and let it cool. The cook accidentally dropped a piece on the ground and after he left, I went over to help myself. Well, you might as well be pecking at a rock, that's how hard it was! Who could eat that? I suppose the sweets looked pretty hanging on the tree since they were colorful, but I think they should just hang worms on the tree instead. Sure, they aren't as pretty, but they're easier to eat, you can just grab one off a branch and pop it in your mouth! I have so many things to work on once I become the sovereign...

While I was watching, I heard a commotion coming from the gardener's shed. That's when I noticed that two of the children were over there investigating that tree. Prince Bertie and young Prince Alfred were there. I knew I had to get over there quickly to protect them in case the squirrels attacked.

I rushed over but then stopped a safe distance away since I knew the littlest prince, Alfred, liked to throw rocks at chickens. As I was lollygagging around, keeping my eye on that tree, those little boys started to wrestle. Bertie was bigger than Afred, but Alfred was a cheeky little bloke and was getting the best of his older brother. I guess Bertie finally had enough of getting trounced by his brother, who was half his size, so he pushed Alfred hard. When Alfred fell he knocked into that tree and it started to wobble a bit from where it was leaning. It slowly started to slide over on its side. It was about to fall on Alfred! As quickly as I could, I let out a warning screech and the gardener, who was working on the stand for the tree, reached out and caught the tree before it fell on top of poor Alfred. I'm sure he would have been hideously maimed by the branches and the hidden squirrels and then no one would have wanted to paint a picture of him for the castle gallery.

Though I didn't know it at the time, my missus had been watching from the library window. She came running outside just in time to help Alfred up and give Bertie a scolding. She glanced at me, but mainly just complimented the gardener on his quick reflexes as she turned, and taking each child in hand, firmly walked away. I was a bit put out because she didn't acknowledge my part in saving her son, but I watched her as she stopped by the back kitchen and had some words with the cook. I saw her turn and nod her head at me before continuing around to the side entrance of the castle. The cook went in the kitchen and came back out with a cranberry scone. Not a burnt scone, like we usually get, but a good one that had been baked that morning. He tossed the whole thing to me! The queen had noticed my devotion to the royal family and asked for me to be rewarded! Before I started to eat, I let out a royal crow because I was sure that giving me a scone that was meant for the family's tea was a sign that I was now a part of the family. I figured that since I saved Alfred's life, that meant I would slide into the line of succession right after

Bertie, making me the spare! My powerful deductive reasoning skills will come in handy when I'm on the throne.

Ever since that day, Christmas has been a favorite time for me. There's a tree branch near the window of the drawing room and every year on Christmas Eve I jump up on that branch and have a look at the Christmas tree. I must admit, those Germans were smart to come up with the idea to bring a tree inside at Christmas. When it's all decorated it's quite a sight to see. Hanging from its branches are colorful sweets as well as small toys and even jewels. There are oranges and pears hung with tiny hooks. There are also small paper cones filled with almonds and raisins resting on the branches. Streamers of colored paper and shiny tinsel hang down from every branch, and underneath the tree are brightly colored packages. The tree has small candles fixed to its branches, of course I've never seen them all lit up, chickens aren't ones to stay up late. But I can imagine how beautiful it must be when the candles light up the room like the very stars in the heavens.

As I stared in the window at my royal family decorating that tree, I sighed in contentment. Christmas is the best time of the year at Windsor Castle. As the sun set, and the shadows creeped onto the lawn I knew it was time to head to the coop for the night. I would just need to take one more close look at that tree and make sure it was safe. I knew my spurs were sharp and ready to protect my missus from a squirrel, if one decided to leap out of the branches at her. After all, we all must do our duty.

Magical Christmas Cheese, Grindelwald, Switzerland, Present Day

C hristmas is all about the cheese. Before the holidays last year, I thought cheese was boring. Every time it showed up in our supper scraps, I would ignore it and peck at something else, but all that's changed. Now cheese is my whole world, but not just any cheese- Magical Christmas Cheese.

My missus calls it raclette, which means the cheese is melted into a liquid. Who knew liquid cheese was so much better than regular cheese? On Christmas Eve last year my missus scorched the raclette and had to start over. I will never forget that frosty afternoon when she trudged through the slush carrying that steaming pot of cheese into our yard. As she dumped the warm cheese onto the ice it hissed and crackled as it settled into the snow. I was the first to dip my beak into that glob of burnt raclette and my life was forever changed. As I sneezed cheese out of my nose, I couldn't help thinking that this was the best day of my life.

For the next week I was able to relive the memories by spending hours preening the cheese out of my neck and chest feathers. Apparently, when it comes to raclette, I'm a messy eater. I even let some of my chicken friends peck the dried cheese out from under my beak since, try as I might, I couldn't make my head twist low enough to reach it myself. I tried to make that crusty, leftover, Magical Christmas Cheese last as long as I could because I knew, sadly, Christmas comes but once a year.

As I suffered through springtime and summer, I counted the days until the weather would get chilly and Christmas would come around again in all its cheesy glory. But what if my missus didn't burn the cheese this year? What if it turned out perfect and I would be denied the one thing that made life worth living? I had to come up with a plan. Imagine how I felt when , and his dumb donkey, almost ruined it all for me.

Here in Switzerland, before we have Christmas, we celebrate Samichlaus Abend first. It's the day on December 6th when Samichlaus wanders out of the woods with his trusty donkey laden with peanuts, cookies, and mandarin oranges for all the good children. As the summer months passed, I had the time to ponder whether getting some cheese from Samichlaus was a possibility. I remembered that if the children wanted treats, they had to sing a song or recite a poem for Samichlaus before he would give them anything. In preparation, I spent the whole month of July perfecting my egg song so it would be ready for my cheese-please performance. But the more I thought about it, the more I doubted that Samichlaus actually had cheese in his bag. If he did, the mandarins, peanuts, and other treats would have been covered in it- I almost fainted when I imagined how delicious a gingerbread cookie smeared with Magical Christmas Cheese would be- but I recovered and concluded that Samichlaus probably didn't carry cheese in his sack.

That's when I came up with my genius plan. Since there was no way I could be sure my missus would burn the cheese this year, I decided I had to bargain with her and trade something for a pot of cheese. I know the one thing she likes as much as raclette on Christmas Eve is Grittibänz. Grittibänz are little men made of bread. I know, it's a bit weird, but she's obsessed with them. She makes dozens of them and gives them out to all her friends and neighbors, and she always makes sure the eyes are made of peanuts. And who has peanuts? Samichlaus of course! I decided that if I could steal peanuts from Samichlaus, I could then use them to trade with my missus for some cheese. What could go wrong?

Schmutzli. That's what could go wrong.

When Samichlaus comes to town, he doesn't come alone, Schmutzli comes with him. Schmutzli wears dark clothes and a hood over his head, probably to cover up his lack of acceptable hygiene. I don't think Schmutzli has had a bath this century. As a chicken, I don't approve of that. Chickens spend a lot of time preening and making sure we're looking our best. That's why people have so much respect for chickens, if you want to be respected you must earn it. Personally, I think Samichlaus should find someone else to carry his bag, after all, you're known by the company you keep. That's why I don't spend time with ducks.

On December 6th I knew Samichlaus had arrived because of the big commotion on the streets. Our town is small, so the arrival of Samichlaus is pretty much the biggest thing that's happened since his arrival last year. I don't usually stray too far out of my yard because my missus doesn't want us getting into trouble scratching around in the neighbor's yard, but since my missus and the whole family were busy inside working on their Advent window, they didn't see me head down the road in search of Samichlaus.

I didn't have far to walk, I heard the Baumgartner children three houses down screeching out a horrible rendition of *Was isch das für es Liechtli?* If they thought they were going to get some candy from Samichlaus with that horrendous noise, they were kidding themselves. If I were Samichlaus I would have covered my ears and escaped back to the woods where I came from. I decided to use the distraction of that ear piercing melody to sneak the peanuts out of the burlap sack.

I was dismayed for a moment when I saw that the sack was still on that dumb donkey's back and Schmutzli seemed to be in charge of reaching in and grabbing treats with his dirty, unhygienic hands. I snuck around to the back of the donkey, something I wouldn't normally do since donkeys tend to kick when someone lurks around behind them, but desperate times call for desperate measures. Luckily, those Baumgarten children seemed to think their singing would improve if they sang that song over and over without ceasing. I waited for the perfect moment, and when Samichlaus looked like he was about to keel over from a massive song-induced migraine I saw Schmutzli leave the donkey's side to check on him. That's when

I flapped my wings as hard as I could and leaped up on the donkey's back.

I expected the donkey to be mildly irritated to have me on his back along with that heavy sack. What I didn't expect was for the donkey to take off running with me riding on top. Since I was as surprised as everyone else, I couldn't think straight and held on to that shaggy donkey's back hair as we sprinted through town leaving a trail of peanuts, cookies, and mandarin oranges behind us. Of course, the Baumgarten children saw this as their opportunity to help themselves to as many of Samichlaus's treats as they could carry, and Schmultzi decided that this was his moment to be relevant, so he chased us down the street, hollering as he went.

I probably haven't mentioned this, but Schmutzli carries a broom made of twigs and when he finally caught up to us, he used that broom to give me the swat of my life. I lost a few feathers on that one, and I put the Baumgarten children to shame with the sounds I made when I landed hard on my bottom, fussing as I ran as fast as I could down the street toward home. I thought I might be able to pick up a bag of peanuts as I ran, but you guessed it, those Baumgarten children had stuffed their shirts, pockets, and mouths with all of Samichlaus's treats.

When I finally made it home, chased by Schmutzli, my missus and the whole family were standing on the porch trying to see what all the commotion was about. When she saw Schmutzli chasing me, she was so mad I thought she was going to hit him with the hand dipped candle she held in her fist, instead, she told Schmutzli to leave me alone and go find his donkey. I think she should have also told him to take a bath, but my missus believes in minding her own business.

That's how my dreams of warm liquid cheese cooling in the Christmas Eve snow ended. Even the sight of the family's Adventsfenster window, with its picture of a brightly colored star shining over the manger scene in Bethlehem didn't cheer me up. Christmas was ruined.

I moped through those next weeks until we woke up Christmas Eve morning to a beautiful dusting of new fallen snow. I could smell all the delicious baking smells coming from the house and I knew my missus was busy making an army of Grittibänz men, but even that wonderful aroma couldn't improve my mood.

As I was scratching through the snow in the back of our yard, I heard my fellow chickens get excited. My missus must be heading our way with some burnt Grittibänz, or a gingerbread cake that turned out a little too toasty. Though I knew that nothing would ever be as good as Magical Christmas Cheese, I didn't want to miss out on a treat, so I plodded through the snow to the front of the coop, then stopped, frozen in my steps.

I saw the sparkle in my missus's eye before I noticed the pot in her hand. She hadn't dumped it out yet, could it be she was waiting for me? Did she somehow know that for the last 364 days of my life I had dreamed of this moment? Without thinking I began to run. I was running so fast that I slid on a patch of ice and ended up slamming into her boots. This made her laugh and with her hand she shooed us back a bit and started to pour. Magical Christmas Cheese for a magical Christmas.

Chicken Tamales and Grasshopper Pinatas, San Miguel de Allende, Mexico, 1950

My abuelita is the best person in the world. She takes good care of all her chickens, but she takes especially good care of me. She calls me her gallinita and in the afternoons, she sits on the patio, and I jump up in her lap. She hums songs and pets me on my neck under my beak and every single time she does that, I fall asleep. I love my afternoon siestas with my abuelita.

Just when I thought life couldn't get any better, I heard the most amazing news yesterday. My missus is busy making all her plans for the Christmas season, she has so many posadas to go to and so many meals to prepare between now and Noche Buena. I thought she was too busy to remember to do something special for the chickens, then I heard her tell abuelita that she was going to make chicken tamales this year. Could that be true? Is she really making a whole batch of tamales just for the chickens? Usually, all we get are the leftovers, I can hardly even imagine having a huge plate of tamales made special for us! My missus is the best!

While my missus and abuelita are busy in the kitchen, my mister and some of the children are out in the yard setting up the rope for the pinata. The posada will be at our house tomorrow night and my mister wants to have everything done ahead of time so it will be perfect. This will be my first posada. Last year the family went to other houses for the celebrations so I'm excited to see one firsthand. From what I've heard, people will come to our house and stand outside and sing a traditional song asking if they can come into the house. They're pretending to be two people called Mary and Joseph. I don't know who Mary and Joseph are, but apparently, they did a lot of wandering around looking for a place to sleep. After my mister lets them in, the party will start! I'm excited for the food and the singing, but I'm definitely not excited for the pinata.

The first time I ever saw a pinata was last year. I was just newly hatched then, and I have to say, what happened to that pinata has traumatized me for life. The pinata was a beautiful star with seven points. My mister said the seven points represent the seven deadly sins. I don't know what a sin is, I'm glad chickens don't sin because if what happened to that pinata is what happens to everyone who sins, I don't want any part of it. I was sitting in the shade enjoying a piece of sopapilla my abuelita had tossed under a chair for me, enjoying the view of that very colorful star with ribbons and streamers hanging down from it. I thought it should stay there in the garden forever, it was that pretty. But then all the children came out of the house and lined up next to the pinata. I knew there were treats inside the pinata, that's why I was out on the patio in the first place. I'm shy and don't like to be around large crowds of people, but I had heard that there would be mandarinas in the pinata and I wanted to get my beak on a juicy, ripe mandarina. Mandarinas are almost as good as snails, they're tough on the outside but juicy on the inside. It takes some work to peck through the shells, but it's more than worth it.

I expected the children to take turns opening the pinata and getting a treat for themselves and one to share with a chicken, but that's not what happened. My mister blindfolded the first child and handed him a stick, then he began to beat that poor, bright, colorful star with the stick! I'm a peace-loving hen, I couldn't stand to see what was happening to that beautiful star. Even though I wanted a mandarina badly, I didn't think I could handle any more violence. Just then, the clay pot inside all that bright tissue paper burst open and all the treats flew everywhere. Well, those children went wild! They scrambled all over the ground picking up treats and filling their pockets and aprons until they couldn't hold any more. I couldn't handle all the commotion, or the sight of the mangled pinata, so I took off running for the safety of the coop.

That's why this year, even though I knew my mister had a whole sack of mandarinas stuffed in the pinata, I was determined to avoid the temptation and stay in the coop where it was safe. At least I was determined until I heard the rumor that this year, for the first time, the pinata would not be in the shape of a star. When I first heard the children talking about it I was excited, I thought it might be nice if the pinata was in the shape of a mandarina, or even a tamale. Then I heard a child say it was going to be an animal. I thought a giant, festive, brightly colored green grasshopper with streamers of worms would make an excellent pinata, but then one of the children said it was going to be an animal that was present at the stable where the baby Jesus was born. That made me think. Did they even have grasshoppers in Bethlehem?

The more I thought about it, the more I knew the pinata wasn't going to be a grasshopper. I went out to the front yard to scratch around the nativity scene my mister had set up and there weren't any grasshoppers there gazing at the manger. So, I knew the pinata would probably be a cow or a sheep, or, and though it made the feathers on my neck stand up in fear, a chicken. I don't think my nerves could handle seeing a chicken pinata beaten to pieces by those violent children the day before Noche Buena. Even though I knew that there were no chickens at my mister's nativity scene in front of our house, that didn't bother me. Of course, chickens would have been there the night baby Jesus was born! Chickens are a very popular animal, everyone in the world knows that. The more I thought about it, the more I convinced myself that the pinata was probably a chicken. A helpless, colorful, tissue paper chicken, hanging by a rope in the yard, just waiting for those horrible children to beat it with a stick! I had to do something, but what?

I knew the pinata was in a small storage shed behind the house, waiting to be hung up in the morning. I also knew that I had to do whatever I could to spare the rest of my chicken family the sight of a chicken pinata getting smashed to pieces. This was my moment to be a hero. I peeked into the shed, there on the floor, I saw something covered with a blanket. I saw a bright piece of red tissue paper peeking out from the bottom of the blanket, so I knew it was the pinata. It was getting late in the afternoon, and I wasn't sure what I was going to do, but I knew I had to try. Maybe if I pulled all the tissue off the pinata it would be too ugly for the children to be interested in it. But first, I had to take that blanket off. I timidly walked slowly towards the blanket and gripped the corner of it with my beak to give it a tug, but before I could put all my energy into it, I heard footsteps. I ran and hid in the corner behind some old pots. It was my mister. He glanced around inside the shed, then pulled the door shut and latched it. Then- silence. I was stuck. Stuck in the lonely shed with that giant, doomed, chicken pinata.

I was so paralyzed with fear I couldn't move. I sat there, behind those pots, unable to even think of what I should do. After some time had passed and I could see the light coming from under the door fading, I heard a voice calling my name. It was my abuelita, she was calling out, "Gallinita! Gallinita!" She was looking for me! She knew I was missing from the coop and cared enough about me to come looking! I should have called out for her, but I was so scared that I couldn't make a sound. Soon, her voice stopped, and the shadows turned to darkness.

I try not to think about my night locked in that shed. I know I slept fitfully, off and on. I think I was scared that the giant chicken pinata would come to life and throw off its blanket and beat me with a stick for all my sins, even though I was still unclear what sins actually were. All I knew was that I had to survive.

When morning came, I was surprised to wake up alive. I was hungry, luckily there were plenty of spiders and beetles running around the shed to snack on. I made a mental note of that in case I wasn't successful finding protein in the outside world I could always come into the shed and see if I could hunt some down. Of course, at other times of the year there wouldn't be an enormous, tissue paper chicken hidden under a blanket to terrify me.

As the day began to get longer, I was beginning to wonder if I was going to have to spend another night with the horror of that pinata, then I finally heard footsteps coming toward the shed. When my mister, accompanied by three of the children, finally opened the door, I was so blinded by the bright sunshine that I ran into the door post as I sprinted out of the shed. I heard my mister call out, "Madre, tu gallinita esta aqui!" I don't know what he said, but I kept running and ran straight into the arms of abuelita, who scooped me up and held me close.

I sat on abuelita's lap that evening, eating small pieces of tortilla out of her hand. The patio was full of people, it seemed like the whole neighborhood must be there. Since I was safe and my tummy was full, I wasn't bothered by the brightly covered pinata gently swinging in the breeze. As it turned out, that pinta wasn't a chicken at all. It was a burro, a symbol of the burro Mary rode on that night long ago when Joseph took her to the inn, looking for a place for her precious child to be born. As the children lined up and my mister brought out that huge stick, I snuggled my head under the feathers of my wings and thought happy thoughts of giant green grasshopper pinatas, and chicken tamales.

The Glorious, Stinky Fish, Tromso, Norway, Present Day

The whole Christmas holiday is ruined for me. I'm so disappointed I can't even lay an egg. It's all because of the terrible news I got yesterday. Yesterday was supposed to be one of the best days of the year because it's the day everyone bakes the Syv Slag, which literally means they bake SEVEN different types of cookies! SEVEN! My missus's family came over and they baked all day. There were plenty of misshapen cookies, and cookies that got a little too toasty, that they tossed to the chickens, that's why we were careful to do our scratching close to the house yesterday. It's because I was scratching right under the kitchen window that I heard my missus make the ominous announcement that this year she wasn't going to be making lutefisk for Christmas dinner. What? How could that be? Lutefisk is a holiday tradition in these parts! Lutefisk is an amazing fish that we only eat at Christmastime, I look forward to it every year! The reason I hop off the roost in the morning is because each new day brings me closer to the annual feast of lutefisk! Lutefisk is special to me and my chicken friends because for some reason there's always a lot of it left over in the plate scrapings and we get to have as much as we want. I can't go without it!

I listened in dismay as I heard my missus telling the others that she simply couldn't stand the smell anymore. She said she hates how the smell gets into the curtains and towels, and even her hair! Chickens don't have hair, but if we did, I would love nothing better than to have my hair smell like the delicious, just-baked lutefisk. The smell is what makes lutefisk exciting! The fact that the smell lingers for days afterwards brings good memories of how wonderful it tasted!

Lutefisk is different from other fish because it jiggles like jam. Jam, by the way, is another one of my favorites, especially lingonberry jam. Sometimes in the breakfast scraps we get pieces of toast that have a bit of jam on them, and I will fight any hen to the death to get some lingonberry jam. In fact, if someone would just come up with the idea to spread some jam on top of the lutefisk that would be world changing.

So, my missus said that instead of serving lutefisk this year, she's going to make a big batch of Syltelabb instead. Syltelabb are pig trotters. Trotters are feet. Don't get me wrong, pig's feet are tasty, but I don't eat them just because I don't think it's fair to the pig. If we eat the pig's feet, how can the pig get around and do whatever it is that pigs do all day? We have a pig here on our farm, her name is Agnes. She's pretty round, maybe if my missus eats her feet we can roll Agnes around from place to place. I would volunteer to help, I'm very strong and if Agnes is pointed in the right direction, I can give

19

her a good shove so she can roll on over to where she needs to go. I like to be helpful, especially at Christmas time.

Back to the tragedy of a Christmas without lutefisk... I've often wondered how lutefisk swim around since they don't seem to have any bones and are so jiggly. Maybe they just ooze around in the water, or maybe they just plop somewhere and stay there for their whole lives. How does one even catch a lutefisk? I don't know but I'm about to find out because if my missus won't do her part to make Christmas festive for all of us, then I will just have to step up and do it myself. I've decided to go fishing.

Though I haven't ever done any fishing myself, I do have some experience with fish. My colleagues and I often wander down to the fjord in the summertime to see if anything tasty has washed up on the shore, also because sometimes the fishermen will clean their fish right there on the shore and fish guts are a protein-filled meal. But when I arrived at the fjord, I didn't see anyone else fishing, probably because it was very cold. I knew I needed a pole and some string and a hook if I was going to fish, so I looked around on the shore but didn't see anything I could use. It occurred to me that I didn't have any hands, and I would have a hard time fishing with my feet since I needed my feet for standing. That's when I gave up on the fishing idea and decided to head to the fish market and see if I could somehow get myself a lutefisk there. The fish market is always crowded, even when it's cold. I stayed at a distance since I didn't want the fish man to throw a fish head at me to get me to leave. Fish heads aren't good eating, except for the eyes. But though I looked at every fish on the table, I didn't see one that resembled a lutefisk at all. They all had bones and were way too solid to be a squishy lutefisk.

With sadness in my heart, I began the long walk home. I trudged past the Julemarked, but even a Christmas market with the smell of freshly made smultringer doughnuts couldn't improve my mood. From my first Christmas, until now, I had always had lutefisk for my holiday dinner, but now all that was over. I would go to bed hungry, with only the memories of that glorious, mushy, stinky fish to fill my empty stomach.

As I came to my street it began to snow. Maybe it was because I was so distracted by the snow that my mind didn't register the smell at first. But as I got closer to home the smell got even stronger. Could it be? I was still so far away, but the unmistakable smell of lutefisk came wafting up the street, filling my nostrils, and my heart, with Christmas joy. Though I was tired from my long walk, I found myself starting to run, so anxious was I to make sure this wasn't some sort of a cruel joke and there really was lutefisk at the end of my journey.

When I arrived at my house I almost fainted both from happiness and from the overpowering toxic smell. From inside the kitchen, I could hear the unmistakable booming voice of my missus's brother Daniel, rising above her protests as he tried to serve her up a second helping of his home-baked lutefisk. I should have known Uncle Daniel would come through for us! I was so excited that I started to fuss. I made the same noise I make when I lay an egg, my happy, excited song announcing to the world that something remarkable has just happened. When the other chickens heard me they all came running and started to sing too. Soon, all twenty-three of us were standing underneath the kitchen window singing for lutefisk. Uncle Daniel didn't disappoint us. His laughing face appeared on the back porch. He tossed us a whole plate of fresh lutefisk that landed on the snow with a *plop* and a *splatter*, and if you think there's anything better than warm lutefisk mixed with newly fallen snow, you're wrong.

That night, as I puffed up my feathers and snuggled in close to another hen on the roost, my tummy was full of lutefisk and my heart was full of Christmas. We have a window in our coop and I went to sleep watching the Northern Lights light up the dark sky while the sounds of Christmas carols and the aroma of lutefisk danced in my dreams.

A Quasimodo Christmas, Meaux, France, Present Day

You know who was completely misunderstood? Quasimodo. Just because Quasimodo wasn't great to look at, people treated him badly. I can relate. I'm not the best-looking hen in our flock, my feathers are patchy and have lost a lot of their shine. Plus, my comb flops over to the side covering one of my eyes so I look a bit like Quasimodo, who had one eye covered by an out-of-control eyebrow. I like to think I have a good heart like Quasimodo did, but unfortunately, people don't take the time to look past my appearance to see my heart. Sometimes I want to run away from home. If I ever ran away, I would go to Paris. In Paris I would be accepted and loved for my brains and my heart. When I go to sleep at night, I dream about Paris, a place where people focus on the important things of life, like croissants and macarons. All people around here care about are eggs, and apparently, I'm not laying enough of them. It's stressful. I know my missus needs extra eggs for her holiday baking, but since when is laying one egg a day not enough? Christmas is supposed to be a wonderful time of the year, but I wish Christmas would just hurry up and get over with already.

Another thing that's been getting me down is our goose. He really thinks he's something. He preens his feathers all day and struts around our farm like he's the best thing since sliced baguettes. I get it, he's handsome. He doesn't have to remind everyone all the time. To make matters worse, I've just heard that the family is going to spend Christmas Eve with their Uncle Maurice in Paris, and guess who's invited? Not me, even though I've always wanted to go to Paris. They've invited the goose because he's bringing foie gras to Uncle Maurice's Réveillon feast. Réveillon is the big Christmas Eve dinner that the family has every year. I don't know where exactly the goose is going to be getting this foie gras, all I know is that every evening after dinner my missus gives the goose all the table scraps, none for us. Apparently, the fatter he is the better the foie gras will be. Maybe he's going to lay foie gras like an egg. All I know is that I'm tired of him acting like he's so special and stuffing his fat face with the family's leftover supper. What about me? I could bring foie gras if someone would just tell me where to get it! And what about all the eggs I lay day after day, year after year? How would my missus make crepes or canapés without eggs? I'm important too, where's my extra table scraps? I hate Christmas.

Since all this was making me grumpy, I decided to try and find a place for a nap. I don't know why, but often after I've taken a nap, the world seems like a much better place. I noticed my mister's bread truck parked in the driveway. My mister and missus run the town boulangerie, so I'm used to seeing the truck parked in our driveway at the end of the day.

I hopped up into the back. It was quiet and dark- perfect for a nap. I scooted in behind a few crates, settled myself down and tucked my head into my not-so-shiny wing feathers and fell asleep

I was having the best nap of my life until I heard the door slam, and the engine start up. Had I slept all through the night and it was morning already? How could that be?

It was hard to keep my footing on the slippery floor as the truck bumped its way over the streets, probably headed for the boulangerie. I wouldn't mind that. I could probably survive for the day on breadcrumbs I found on the floor of the truck. But why was this ride taking so long? I knew the boulangerie was just in the town square, not too far from our house, but this ride was taking forever!

When the truck finally came to a stop, I expected my eyes to be blinded by the light when the doors opened, but it was already late in the afternoon, so the sky was dim. I waited until my mister got done carrying crates out, then I quietly walked over and hopped out. That's when I saw Christmas.

There were illuminations everywhere, strings and strings of fairy lights and shiny, blinking stars! The street was lined with brightly colored stalls selling all sorts of treats and gifts. There was so much to look at I didn't know where to start, but before I could take a step, I was startled by the loud chimes coming from the building rising up in the semi-darkness beyond the street. Could it be the Cathedral of Notre Dame? Was I really and truly in Paris? I looked through the twilight to see if I could spy Quasimodo up there, yanking on the ropes that made the bells ring to mark the hour. Quasimodo, a kindred spirit, misunderstood and abused by society as I was. But I wasn't going to think about that tonight, I was here at the Marché de Noel Notre Dame, and I was going to enjoy every moment.

I snuck around the back of a stall and decided to head out to the main section so I could see all the treats and wares that were for sale. I saw a small chalet selling cashmere scarves and I thought those would be good for our nesting boxes since our straw can get a bit scratchy on our delicate bottoms. The next time my missus asked me what I wanted for a Christmas gift I would definitely tell her a cashmere scarf for my nesting box. Oh wait, she's never asked me what gift I wanted for Christmas!

No negative thoughts! I'm in Paris!

The next stall was one of my favorites- escargot! Snails have always been a favorite of mine, but I disapprove of people cooking them. Snails are best enjoyed raw and slimy, it makes them go down easier. But beggars can't be choosers, and I was hungry, so I was happy to find myself an escargot that had dropped on the ground. It was a bit stale, but tasty, nonetheless. Maybe it was because I was concentrating on my dinner that I didn't notice a man walking straight toward me. I looked up just in time to avoid getting trampled by Père Noël himself! He was just strolling down the street, drinking a cup of Vin Chaud and being followed by a gaggle of adoring children. I don't drink Vin Chaud myself because every year I hear my missus shouting about how Uncle Maurice always ruins Christmas for everyone when he's been drinking too much mulled wine. No one wants to be like Uncle Maurice. When Père Noël saw me, he tossed me a roasted chestnut from a packet he was holding. To think I actually got to meet Père Noël on the streets of Paris! I knew everyone back home would be jealous when they heard about this!

Home. Suddenly I started to feel a bit homesick. Chickens aren't big travelers, and it was getting dark. I thought of my cozy place in the barn and how nice it would be to be there now with my chicken friends, settling down for the night. I was about to turn back to try and find my mister's boulangerie stall when I heard some people talking. They were talking about a stall at the end of the market, a stall that sold foie gras. That irritated me because I had been having the best time and had managed to forget about that fat faced goose and his foie gras that he was going to give the family, but then, what I heard made me stop in my tracks. One mademoiselle was telling the other mademoiselle that she refused to eat foie gras because the poor goose has to die so that his liver can be turned into foie gras! Die? Were they really going to kill our goose and chop his liver out of him? Suddenly I remembered the story- how Quasimodo tried to save Esmerelda from a terrible death! Of course, he failed and didn't save her and, in the end, she ended up getting hanged. But that was just a story for children, it was Christmas, and my story hadn't been written yet! Maybe I could save the goose from a Christmas tragedy! I had to warn him!

I rushed back to my mister's truck and got there just in time. They were packing up for the night and I was able to hop-fly into the back and find my place behind the crates before they shut the door. I tried to stay awake, I knew that goose was in trouble, and he didn't even know it. I was his Quasimodo, and he was my Esmerelda, it was up to me to save him. I wanted to stay awake and think up a plan, but I was so tired I fell asleep. I never even heard when we came to a stop in our driveway and my mister headed into the house. I slept all through it-slept while the far away bells of Notre Dame tolled mournfully into the night.

My mister was certainly surprised when he opened the back of the truck in the morning and I flew out. My left wing grazed his cheek as I flew, I'm not very good at steering while I fly, but I left him an egg behind the crate, so I felt like that made up for the inconvenience.

I ran as fast as I could, my eyes searching everywhere for that goose. Was I too late? Had he already been turned into foie gras, his quivering liver sitting in a refrigerator in the house awaiting the drive to Uncle Maurice's house and the Réveillon feast? I was running so fast that when I turned the corner of the barn I almost ran straight into my missus and her daughter. The daughter was crying, and my missus was kneeling on the ground hugging her. I didn't understand all of what they said but basically my missus was promising not to make the goose into foie gras since the daughter loved him as a pet. My dreams of a heroic rescue were over, the goose was saved, and the family decided to bring raw oysters to Uncle Maurice's instead of foie gras. Raw oysters, yuck.

While my missus walked her young daughter back up to the house I followed them. Through the open door I could see the crèche displayed on the tabletop near the window. I didn't see any chicken santons in the scene, just a cow, some sheep, and a pig. There was also a fisherman, a baker, a washerwoman, and a butcher. The family liked to go all out when it came to nativity scenes. Even though there were no chickens and not a single goose, it still made me happy to see all the people who were there to celebrate the baby Jesus coming into the world. As I turned to head back toward the barn, I thought about my Paris adventure. I may not have gotten the chance to be a hero, but I did get to see how beautiful Paris is at Christmas time, and that's something I'll always remember.

Straw Goats and a Cartoon Duck, Forsby, Sweden, Present Day

I t's almost Christmas and I'm running out of time to make the changes that need to be made in order to make Christmas in Sweden the best that it can be. I know it's almost Christmas because as I was settling down to sleep up on the roost, I could see through the window of our coop that the family was dressed up and getting in the car. The three daughters were dressed in beautiful white dresses with red sashes around their waists. The two youngest girls had wreaths of evergreen branches on their heads and the oldest one had a wreath with four candles. I've seen enough Christmases to know that they were dressed for the Saint Lucia church service.

I'm not sure who Saint Lucia was, but from what I've heard she was a very kind girl who did good deeds for others. When the family arrives at church, they'll light the candles on the oldest girl's wreath, and everyone will think that it's very beautiful. I think it's a fire hazard. I would hate for her hair to catch on fire, I think her head will get chilly this time of the year if she doesn't have any hair. I hope chickens never start celebrating Saint Lucia, I wouldn't want my feathers to catch on fire. I would be cold if I were naked in the wintertime.

All this means that there are less than two weeks left until Christmas. So, I'm running out of time to make a better holiday for all of us. I believe strongly in being a hen of action. Instead of complaining about the things that need fixing, I need to take steps to fix them. The first thing I need to deal with is the goats.

I don't know why Swedes are so fascinated with goats at Christmas time, I mean, goats get up every morning and accomplish exactly-nothing. Goats don't even lay eggs, and yet, every house has a straw goat on the porch and all the Christmas trees have straw goat ornaments. Goats aren't even made of straw! I've heard that there's a town not far from here where they have a straw goat as big as a house. One year someone burned that straw goat to the ground so there was nothing left. Probably it was one of those Saint Lucia girls who got too close to it when her candles were lit.

I think most people like goats because Jultomten uses a goat to pull his cart of presents. He likes to wander around and give gifts to all the children on Christmas Eve. Jultomten is kind of like Santa Claus. But honestly, why doesn't Jultomten just use a car to take his presents around? Or maybe even a truck? Goats aren't an efficient way to deliver presents. That's why I must help everyone see that goats aren't a good Christmas tradition. I don't think I have time to deal with all the goats on all the porches in all of Sweden, but I can start with the goat on our own front porch.

When I woke up in the morning, I waited until the children went to school and my mister and missus went to work. Then I hopped up on the porch and had a good look at our straw porch goat. He had a festive ribbon around his neck, but other than that he was boring. I pecked him a couple of times and tried to pull some of his straw out, but he was solidly built and the best I could do was pull at his bow until it came undone. I'm not, by nature, a very devious hen, so I didn't have any great ideas. I just knew I had to do something. So, I ran at that goat and flapped my wings and flew into it with my legs outstretched. It took a couple of tries, but eventually I was able to knock it right off the porch where it fell into the mud. I was exhausted, but I made my point.

The next morning, I decided to head out to the front of our house so I could do my scratching and check on that goat. It was hard to scratch around since it had snowed that night. I saw the goat right where I kicked him, covered in ice and mud. I also saw my missus standing on the porch looking down at it. She looked sad. That made me feel guilty. It was a bad thing that I had done. My missus is a good missus. She loves her Christmas decorations, and I ruined her giant porch goat. For sure no one would ever want to put Saint Lucia candles on my head, I was a terrible chicken.

After that I spent the rest of the time until Christmas moping and trying to figure out a way to undo the bad deed I had done. Jultomten didn't usually bring gifts to chickens, but in case he decided to think of us this year, I didn't want to be left out because of what I did to that goat. The only trouble was, there was another Swedish tradition that I really needed to deal with. It involves ducks, one duck in particular.

Every year, at 3:00 on Christmas Eve, the whole country sits down in their living rooms to watch a Christmas show about a cartoon duck. Last year I flew up on a tree branch so I could look through the window to see why this duck was such a big deal. I can honestly say that I don't know what the fuss is all about. First, he doesn't even look like a real duck. Ducks don't wear clothes, but if they did, why would they wear a shirt but no pants? Secondly, he doesn't sound like a real duck because ducks can't talk. Why on earth does everyone think he's so great? And why didn't somebody make a Christmas cartoon about a chicken instead of a duck? Chickens are much more interesting, and we aren't anywhere near as messy as ducks! It's just irritating. I have to find a way to show the world that ducks are no good. I'll start with the ducks in my own backyard.

We share our coop with three ducks and a goose. Every morning my missus brings us fresh water because our water usually freezes at night. A nice, cold drink of water right after you wake up is so refreshing, but I never get to experience it because the ducks and the goose are obsessed with water! They run right over and stick their whole heads in the tub and bite at the water. Then they try to get in the tub and dirty it up with their dirty feet. And once, and I know this is hard to hear, once I saw a duck relieve himself in our drinking water! It's true! I guess that's why the cartoon duck doesn't wear pants.

In order to stop my family from watching the cartoon duck I needed to show them how terrible ducks really are. So, on Christmas Eve morning, when my missus came out to bring us our water, I hid behind a bale of hay and waited for the exact right moment. As soon as she put that tub down and the ducks started jumping in, I snuck up behind one as he waddled past and pecked him hard on his rear- he squawked and jumped straight up. He landed in the tub with all his weight and splashed the icy water all over my missus, it even got into her hair. She screamed and was so startled she jerked a foot back, hit an icy spot, and fell hard on her backside. My mister heard her scream and came running. He helped her up. She didn't look like she was hurt, but she didn't look happy either. I think she had done her hair specially for Christmas Eve and now it was all ruined with dirty duck water. I felt terrible. I didn't mean for that to happen.

Later that afternoon when the grandparents and aunts and uncles came over to feast on the julbord I stayed in the coop, in the corner by myself. I knew my missus would bring some scraps out to all of us when they were done, but even the thought of meatballs, pickled herring, and saffron buns didn't make me happy, I knew I wasn't worthy. I resigned myself to going to bed without any julbord treats as a punishment for what I had done. Even though I had the best of intentions and just wanted to make Christmas the best that it could be, I hadn't stopped to think about what others wanted. Maybe my family liked the straw goats and the cartoon duck show. Is it possible that Christmas was already the best it could be?

It gets dark early in Sweden this time of the year. As I sat alone in the semi-darkness, I could hear the rest of the flock clucking and squabbling over the julbord scraps my missus brought for us. And even though the house is on the other side of the yard from our coop, I could hear through the walls the sound of children laughing. I knew they were watching that pants-less cartoon duck.

I sat dejectedly looking at the floor, but then I heard footsteps. I looked up and there, in the doorway, was my missus with a plate in her hand. She smiled at me and made a clucking sound which I knew meant to come over to her. She knelt and dumped a small dish of Ris à lá malta on the hay covered floor. Rice pudding is my absolute favorite, did she know that? As I started eating the strawberry that was on the top, I wondered why my missus would bring me something so good when I had been so bad. Maybe my missus was really Saint Lucia herself, or maybe my missus was just an ordinary person who knew the power of forgiveness. As I pecked away at my treat, I found something hard in the pudding, it was an almond. The Swedish tradition says the one who finds the almond in the pudding will get married sometime in the next year. Married! Who wants to get married? What a dumb tradition! I'll have to deal with it next year...

The Christmas Pickle, Berrien Springs, Michigan, USA, Present Day

As far as I'm concerned, a pickle is a waste of a good cucumber. Cucumbers are tasty and they smell good. You have to peck at them for a while to get to the soft inside, but chickens like a challenge and pecking a hole in a cucumber so you can have a delicious lunch is one of my favorite summertime activities. I'm not sure why my missus gets so mad about it, I only eat a little of the cucumber. There's still plenty left for her.

I'm what they call a "French hen." That means I'm the most beautiful hen in the whole flock. I know this because I once heard my missus say that all the most beautiful fashions and hats come from France. Chickens don't wear hats, but if we did, I would definitely wear a hat from France. But it's not just my beauty that makes me better than the other hens, it's the fact that I'm famous that makes me stand out from the rest. You see, I'm featured in one of the most popular Christmas songs there is.

My mister and missus's children are very fond of singing, especially nowadays since it's almost Christmas. They wander all over the yard singing various Christmas carols, that's how I found out that I'm in a song. It's kind of an irritating song since it repeats the verses over and over and you have to remember all the parts. It's a song about a missus who receives some crazy gifts from her true love. On the third day of Christmas her true love gives her three French hens! That is one lucky lady to have a mister who loves her enough to give her not one, not two, but THREE French hens!

Of course, I know that the mister also gives her some other birds such as a partridge in a pear tree, geese, swans, and four calling birds- what on earth is a calling bird? But of all those birds, the French hens are the best. The reason for it is because we lay eggs, and another Christmas tradition is eggnog, you can't have eggnog without eggs! I know those other birds lay eggs too, but do you really want to slurp down a festive mug of goose egg eggnog? Or have yourself a Christmas morning swan egg omelet? Or maybe bake some gingerbread with partridge in a pear tree eggs? I rest my case.

Being the prettiest hen in the flock comes with responsibilities. I must be a leader and help the other hens, and the family, do the right thing. That's why I need this tradition of ruining cucumbers to stop. Sometimes in the dinner scraps my missus will toss us some sliced pickles. No self-respecting chicken will eat a pickle. We always leave them for the squirrels, but the squirrels won't touch them either. Who knew squirrels had self-respect? I even saw the cat give a pickle a sniff then run away fast. Why is it that the animals know that pickles are bad, but humans don't?

But wait, it gets worse. I've just learned that the family actually hangs a slimy, old pickle on their Christmas tree! I don't know much about Christmas trees but from what I can see through the window, the Christmas tree is a beautiful, colorful, symbol of all that is wonderful about Christmas. Hanging a pickle on a lovely fir tree is just wrong.

I heard my missus telling the little ones the legend of the Christmas pickle. She said that long ago there was something called a Civil War. During this war a mister was captured and sent to prison. He was so hungry that he begged a guard to give him some food. That guard gave him a pickle from his lunch, and it saved his life. Did he give him half his sandwich? No, just a pickle. Gee, thanks!

Another story my missus told involved St. Nicholas himself. St. Nicholas is the fancy way of saying "Santa Claus." She said long ago a wicked man grabbed two boys and shoved them in a barrel of pickles. St. Nicholas saved them from the terrible death that would have come to them from breathing pickle fumes. I don't believe this story at all because I know Santa Claus would have the good sense to be as far away from a barrel of pickles as he could get.

No matter which story is true, the children seem to like the whole pickle tradition because whoever is first to find the pickle on the Christmas tree on Christmas morning gets an extra present. That's a little bit greedy if you ask me. And also, why hang a pickle? Wouldn't a cucumber work just as well? If they were hanging a tasty cucumber on the tree, I wouldn't have a problem at all.

So, it's up to me to save the family from having their house, and their breath, smelling like pickles on Christmas morning. That means I have to get inside the house somehow. It shouldn't be too hard, the cat and the dog go in and out of the house, why can't I?

There's a potted plant on our porch. I'm familiar with it because sometimes I like to lay an egg in it. I decided to hop up there and hide and wait for my moment to get in the house. The first day, I spent the whole day in that plant but never got the chance to run in the door. The second day my opportunity came. The dog scratched at the door and my missus opened it for him, since she was in a hurry, when she shut the door it didn't quite latch. With a little nudge, I was in.

This was my first time in the house, it was very different from our chicken coop. For starters, there wasn't any hay on the floor. Hay is important, I wonder why the family doesn't want hay? But I couldn't waste time thinking about that, I had to find the Christmas tree and get that pickle off of it while I had the chance.

I turned a corner and there it was- the most beautiful thing I have ever seen. This must be the living room, the room I could see through the window from the outside. I stopped short because that tree was even more lovely up close. It was covered in brightly colored glass ornaments and had lights on a string twinkling from its branches. I could have stood there forever just looking at it, but I knew it was only a matter of time before someone caught me in the house. Though I'm a fancy French hen, that's never been enough for an invitation to join the family in the living room.

I stood in front of the tree and scanned it for a pickle. I saw glass stars and brightly colored balls with etched pictures on them. I saw glass fruits and vegetables, but no pickles anywhere. Then I remembered that the pickle has to be hidden on the tree for a child to find it. I needed a closer look.

I hopped up on an upholstered chair, then I hopped from the seat to the arm of the chair so I could get a better look. It took a few minutes before I saw it, and when I did, I had to look for a long time at it because, to my astonishment, that pickle was beautiful. It wasn't a real pickle, it wasn't slimy and smelly. It was a glass pickle, it was the most beautiful green color, darker than a cucumber, and it had a little bow tied to the hook. My plan had been to take the pickle and run out the door with it and destroy it to save the family from their own bad judgment. But this pickle was too shiny and sparkly to destroy. I had to admit to myself that it was very possible that I had been wrong about the Christmas pickle tradition.

I was so mesmerized with the shiny glass pickle ornament that I didn't notice the dog. He had wandered into the living room and froze when he saw me. Then, predictably, he did what he does best, bark. That dog barks at everything. If a leaf falls from a tree, he barks. If it starts to rain, he barks. If he notices he has a tail, he twists his neck around and barks at it. Though he's not the brightest creature who ever walked the earth, he knew that even a French hen didn't belong in the living room, and he let the whole world know. I squawked and flapped my wings and flew down from that chair and was out the front door without even leaving a feather behind. I heard my missus scold the dog for barking at nothing. That's what he gets for not minding his own business.

On Christmas morning we were up scratching around looking for some yuletide worms for our breakfast when we heard the children squeal with delight at the sight of their full stockings and the many presents under the tree. I heard my mister announce to them that no one could touch a present until someone finds the pickle. It didn't take long before I heard the joyous call of "I found it" while everyone else laughed and exclaimed their congratulations. Maybe I've gone soft in my old age, but it seems to me that the Christmas pickle is a tradition that the whole family enjoys. Who am I to judge? I suppose even a French hen can be wrong every once in a while.

Crazy for Reindeer, Rovaniemi, Lapland, Finland, Present Day

This whole town is reindeer crazy. That's all anyone cares about. Every year thousands of people come to visit us, and they all want to pet the reindeer and take a ride on a sled drawn by reindeer. Why this fascination with reindeer? Well, it's all because of this misinformed American poet who lived a long time ago. He wrote a poem about the night before Christmas. In his poem he says that Santa's sleigh was drawn by "eight tiny reindeer." Are you kidding me?

I know a lot about reindeer because reindeer have been a big part of life here in the Arctic Circle for centuries. The first thing to know is that reindeer are not tiny. They're huge. Huge and shaggy. And they smell bad, really bad. They aren't trustworthy at all and to even suggest that a smart man like Santa Claus would consider letting reindeer lead his sleigh is preposterous. Of course there's the other glaring problem- reindeer can't fly! I've known enough reindeer in my life to know this is true. Reindeer stomp around in the snow, they don't fly through the night sky bringing joy to the children of the world. It's all such lies.

Apparently, according to the American poet, Santa's reindeer even have names. He said their names were Dasher, Dancer, Prancer, Vixen, Comet, Cupid, Dunder, and Vixen. Honestly, could they have dumber names? My mister runs a sleigh ride business for the tourists and our reindeer are named Arvo and Igor. Now those are good names- strong Finnish names! Though Arvo is a little slow witted and never seems to know what's going on, Igor is an excellent example of a Lapland reindeer. Igor is tough and sturdy. He likes to gallop around our farm and get his exercise. He knows our mister counts on him to be ready to pull a sleigh of tourists through the fresh fallen snow at a moment's notice. My point is, if you were Santa, who would you rather trust to pull your heavy sleigh on the most important night of the year? Someone with a wimpy name like Prancer, or someone with an athletic name like Igor?

Of course I'm worked up about all this because I don't understand why that poet chose reindeer for his poem instead of chickens. I know, I know, chickens can't exactly fly either, but we're a lot better at flying than reindeer are! I'm proud of my flying abilities. I can't soar over the rooftops, but I can get off the ground and fly from the coop to the back porch when my missus has the dinner scraps ready for us. And chickens are much better looking than reindeer, we also have better hygiene. We keep our feathers preened and we control our bodily odors a whole lot better than reindeer. I'm tired of all the attention reindeer get around here, chickens are always ignored and taken for granted. And since I mentioned the supper scraps, you know what's extra tasty? Reindeer steak! Put that in a poem!

It's almost Christmas and I've decided that instead of spending so much time complaining about all this I'm going to do something about it. Tonight is Christmas Eve and when Santa shows up, I'm going to have a conversation with him and suggest that he replace the reindeer with chickens and let us have a go at it. He could put a harness on about twenty of us and hook us to his sleigh and I'm sure we would do a great job and be much quicker and more efficient than the reindeer, plus we smell better. That's got to be rough on Santa to be riding back behind those reindeer– if you know what I mean. If he's worried about the poem, we can just rewrite that line from the poem. Instead of saying:

When what to my wondering eyes did appear
But a miniature sleigh and eight tiny reindeer
We could say:
When what to my wondering eyes I saw kickin'
But a miniature sleigh and twenty full sized chickens!

It's a compelling argument and I will be ready to state the facts when Santa shows up tonight. As for now, the sun is finally out, which means I have about two and a half hours to get some scratching done before it gets dark again. Unfortunately, Arvo and Igor are out munching on grass in my favorite scratching spot. Those reindeer are wearing on my last nerve. Now I have to find another place. I decided to head over to the sauna since the family were all done with their Christmas Eve morning sauna time and had gone into the house to watch the peace declaration on television. The sauna is a mystery to me, everyone goes in there and gets very hot and sweaty. It doesn't look refreshing to me. Last year, my mister's cousin was drinking too much gløgg while he was in the sauna and came out without his towel or his shoes. My missus wasn't happy about that. I think she was worried that he would get cold since he doesn't have feathers like a chicken.

I was so distracted by my daydreams of pulling Santa's sleigh that I didn't notice that I had somehow offended Argo. Like I said, Argo isn't the smartest reindeer you'll ever meet. I looked up to see him charging at me. Maybe he thought I was a pile of grass, and he was hungry, I am a very pretty straw-colored hen, but since there's no reasoning with Argo, I did the only thing I could do- run. I started to squawk and fuss and run full speed without even looking where I was going. I'm a fast runner but I only have two feet, Argo has four. I knew I had to do something quick, or I would be smashed into the ground and never get the chance to lead Santa's sleigh through the starry night sky. The sauna was directly in front of me and luckily, someone had left the door open a crack, so I slid in and skidded in on the slippery floor. As I was catching my breath I heard an unmistakable click. The door shut behind me. I was locked in.

Being locked in the sauna was not ideal. Since the steam had been turned off, it was starting to get chilly, and I knew that when the sun went down it would get downright cold and I had no other hens to snuggle up with. I looked around, there was no hay, no discarded towels, not even a warm cup of gløgg to get me through the night. Besides, how would Santa find me if I was in the sauna and not in the coop where I belonged? This was the worst Christmas ever.

One thing chickens are good at is pacing. When my missus forgets to let us out of our yard, I make sure to pace around in front of the fence until she remembers. Since pacing is one of my best skills, I started to pace around inside the sauna. Too bad it was so dark no one could see me. Then, I started to fuss and pace at the same time. Multi-tasking is also a good skill of mine. Unfortunately, I don't think anyone heard me because they were all so busy in the house eating their Christmas Eve dinner of ham and Christmas boxes. Oh no! I was missing out on the Christmas dinner scraps! Christmas boxes are my absolute favorite! My missus always cooks one that is made of smashed up carrots, there is absolutely nothing better than carrots mashed into mush! I could probably survive a night in the sauna, but there was no surviving a Christmas without a carrot mush Christmas box casserole!

There was nothing I could do but wallow in despair. I slumped down on the floor and sank into a deep depression. About two minutes later I heard a thumping on the door. One whole side of the sauna is glass so my family can enjoy being warm and sweaty while watching the snow fall outside. The family is odd. Through the glass I could see a reindeer. Was Argo still hunting me? Was it still his dream to pound me into a chicken mush casserole for his Christmas box dinner? But it wasn't Argo, it was Igor! Even though Argo and Igor look exactly the same, Igor has a problem digesting his food, and I could smell him even through the thick sauna walls. It was definitely him. He was pawing at the door, trying to help me! Reindeer are the best creatures ever! Igor continued to paw and bellow until I heard footsteps coming down the path from the house. It was my missus, all bundled up and wondering why Igor was making such a racket. When she opened the door and I bolted out, she was astonished to say the least. I ran full speed ahead to the chicken coop and was never so happy to see my chicken friends as I was right then.

I slept on the roost that night, warm and safe. I missed seeing Santa, but I was good with that. I was rethinking the idea of leading Santa's sleigh. Igor had shown me that reindeer were more than just strength and body odor- they were kind and concerned about others. I owed Igor my life and I wanted him to have the chance to lead Santa's sleigh as his reward. Besides, if I were out too late on Christmas Eve night delivering presents, I might miss out on the Christmas boxes, and that's something I simply couldn't risk.

May I Have Some Pierogi Please, Poznań, Poland, Present Day

I have a secret. If everything goes according to my plan I'll be sleeping in the house with the family tonight instead of out in the chicken coop with everybody else. I hope I'll get to sleep in the bed with Grandfather Kasper, he's my favorite. He's the one who told the story last year that showed me how I could become a part of the family. I think he knew I was listening. I think he wanted me to hear because we're best friends and he can spend more time with me if I'm in the house with him. I'm excited, but there's still a lot that has to happen before I can become a real part of the family.

Tonight is what we call Wigilia, which means the family will have a feast for Christmas Eve. Chickens don't have calendars to keep track of the days but I know tonight is Wigilia because the children came out to the barn to grab a handful of hay. They always borrow some of our hay to put on their dinner table. They say it's a symbol of Baby

Jesus being born in a manger. I think it's the only time of the year the family eats hay.

Since we know tonight is the Wigilia feast we're all anxious for the after dinner table scraps. Wigilia has not one, not two, but TWELVE dishes for the family to feast on. They never eat meat, always fish and vegetable dishes. Pierogi is always my favorite. Pierogi is a dumpling stuffed with mushrooms. Last year there was a whole half of a dumpling in the scraps and I was the one to get it! I ran away as fast as I could with three hens chasing close behind. I hid in the barn under the cow and those hens couldn't find me so I got to eat the whole pierogi all by myself. Merry Christmas to me!

After dinner Grandfather Kasper always plays his accordion. He plays so well that my missus only let's him play on very special occasions. I think she's afraid if he plays too often all the songs he knows will run out of his head and he won't have anything left to play on special days like Wigilia. She also says that he can only play one or two songs at the most, probably because she wants to save some songs for next time. I like to hear Grandpa Kasper play the accordion, it reminds me of chasing a grasshopper through a field and then suddenly stepping in a gopher hole and falling down, then getting back up to chase some more.

Back to my plan. Every year the family has a Christmas tradition of sharing an oplatek with those they love. An oplatek is a wafer. You're supposed to break off a piece from a loved one's wafer and wish them a Happy Christmas while you do it. I know all about it because every year Grandfather Kasper always saves an oplatek for the chickens, but it wasn't until after Christmas last year that I found out the real reason grandfather always saves some oplatek for us. He says, that according to legend, if animals eat oplatek on Christmas Eve, at midnight they will be able to talk. So, if I can stay up until midnight, I will be able to talk! Surely any chicken who can have a conversation with regular words wouldn't have to live in the barn with the cows any more! The oplatek is my ticket into the family where I will be able to sit at the dinner table every night and eat as much pierogi as I want. It will be a Christmas miracle!

All year long I have been thinking about what my life will be like once I'm living in the house. I wonder if I'll miss my chicken friends? I wonder what kind of bugs I'll find when I'm scratching in the house, maybe they have bugs in there that chickens have never even seen before! I wonder what it will be like to sleep in Grandpa Kasper's bed and lay eggs on his nice clean sheets? I think my missus will like that part, she won't have to walk to the barn to get some eggs to make the dumplings for the pierogi. I've sat on my roost many nights this past year with dreams of my new life lulling me to sleep.

It's getting late and I can hear the festivities in the house winding down. I know as soon as they're done with dinner and gifts, they'll go to church for a midnight mass. It's when they return from church that I plan to meet them at the front door and tell them in the human language that I'm ready to come inside. I'll be sleepy at midnight, so I'll be sure and ask my missus if she can find an extra pillow for me. I know Grandfather Kasper won't mind sharing his bed with me, I just think it would be more polite if I had my own pillow.

In the meantime, I decided to hop up on a tree branch on the side of the house where I can see directly into the dining room. The family is sitting there eating their dessert of , which looks delicious. I'll be sure to remember to save some room for that next year!

50

As I sit and try to keep my eyes open I can see the extra place set at the table right next to Grandfather. I know they do this every year, it's supposed to be in case someone unexpected shows up for dinner. I think next year I will invite one of my hen friends to come to dinner and sit in that place. I'm sure I'll want to share my good fortune with everyone. That thought made me kind of sad. I know I'll miss my chicken friends. I'll miss chasing after each other when one of us catches something good to eat. I'll miss the sound of our rooster crowing in the morning to wake us up, and I'll miss the clicking noises my missus makes when she's bringing us the supper scraps.

While I was thinking about all this I fell asleep, still perched in that tree. Chickens don't stay up late, so even though this was the most important night of my life I couldn't help myself. I fell asleep to the sound of the children opening presents and Grandfather Kasper playing the accordion. I don't know how long I slept, but I woke up when Grandfather gently lifted me out of the tree and carried me to the barn. I knew it was time to open my beak and speak the Polish words that would shock Grandfather and cause him to race with me into the house to show everyone that I had learned to talk. But I was so sleepy, I couldn't make a sound.

Grandfather placed me on the roost and I settled down with the rest of my chicken family. Maybe I had two families, a chicken family and a human family. The truth was, I had a good life the way things were and I didn't want to risk messing that up by changing everything. Besides, tomorrow morning my missus would bring us the Wigilia table scraps and I felt sure that there was a pierogi in that feast that was meant only for me. Maybe next year was the year I would stay up until midnight and speak the words that would change everything, or maybe, things were good just the way they were. Wesołych Świąt!

Being Good is Hard to Do, Rome, Italy, Present Day

I've been so good. Well, I've been mostly good, but the real question is, have I been good enough? The problem with being good here in Italy is that the Christmas holidays stretch on forever, it's hard to be good forever! I only made one rather minor mistake, but surely it wasn't bad enough to keep me from getting treats in my stocking, I very much want to get my treats!

Some may think that I'm waiting on Santa, or, as we call him here, Babbo Natale, to bring me some goodies, but that's not who I'm waiting for at all. Babbo Natale is competent as far as gifts go, but the really special treats come from La Befana and she doesn't get here until January 6th! See what I mean about having to be good for a long time?

La Befana is a kindly old lady who rides around on a broomstick bringing sweets and small gifts to all the well-behaved children.

Somehow, she knows who's been good, and who's been bad. If you've been bad, you get a lump of coal in your stocking instead of the candy and toys. I don't know what a lump of coal is, but it seems to me that anything that comes in a "lump" probably isn't very good. Unless maybe, it's a lump of grasshoppers, or maybe a lump of worms. I wouldn't mind getting a tasty lump of worms!

The big problem is that La Befana leaves these surprises in the children's stockings. Chickens don't wear socks. I thought of trying to get a sock somewhere, maybe I could sneak one out of my missus's laundry basket when she's hanging out the clothes to dry. But again, I'm trying to be good and stealing a sock would be bad. I just have to believe that La Befana knows all about chickens and our lack of footwear. Maybe she could leave my treats in the nesting box, that's the perfect place!

The month started out well, December 8th is when the Christmas season starts here in Rome. Since I'd heard so much about La Bafana and her job of leaving treats for well-behaved chickens (and children) I decided I had to do something really special so she would notice me, so I came up with the best idea ever. My epic plan was to secure a place in the Presepi Viventi in the town piazza. A Presepi Viventi is a living nativity scene and since I knew my mister was in charge of the animals, I thought I had a great chance of being chosen and showing our whole town what a good chicken I was. Maybe La Befana would be in the crowd and would see me and put me on her list for a lump of caterpillars!

In the weeks leading up to the Presepi my mister's teenage son Alessandro would come out to our coop and practice holding various ones of us so he could see who would be tame enough to be involved.

54

Most chickens aren't fond of being held, me included, but since I had so much at stake I was determined that Alessandro would pick me. Every day I ran right up to him and when he picked me up, I would sit calmly in his arms trying to show him that I deserved a place in the Presepi.

As the days went by, I started to get more anxious because I could tell it was almost time. Alessandro and his younger brothers were practicing walking sheep around on ropes, and a lady from the town came over to our house and practiced riding our donkey, Bruno. I don't think Bruno liked her very much, he sure made a lot of noise when she sat down. Maybe Bruno doesn't know how important it is to be good this time of the year.

Finally, the morning I had been waiting for arrived. Alessandro, dressed as a shepherd, came out to the coop and scooped me up. We walked to the piazza with his brothers leading the sheep and took our places in the Presepi. As I looked around at all of us, I was proud to be a part of this wonderful scene. Alessandro and his brothers were the shepherds, I saw three misters dressed up as kings, and a missus and a mister kneeling on the straw with a real live baby in the wooden manger. Of course, all of the animals were there, sheep, goats, Bruno, a cow, and me, the one and only chicken!

Crowds of people pressed in to see us, it was a little scary to be around so many strangers, but Alessandro held me against his chest and stroked the feathers on my neck. He talked soothingly to me and it wasn't long before I was completely relaxed. I was just about to take a little nap and dream about the treats that La Befana would bring me, when suddenly, I felt it start to happen.

I'd been so stressed about being a part of the Presepi that I hadn't laid an egg in days, maybe a week. Perhaps it was because I was feeling so calm that an egg decided it was time to come out. I can't exactly stop it when it starts, but I did know that this was definitely not the best time to be laying an egg. I decided to concentrate my hardest on trying to keep that egg inside me until it was time to go home. I shut my eyes and gritted my beak, but just when I was starting to feel in control, suddenly, behind me, a booming, howling noise startled me half to death!

It was the zampognari! Of course, I knew the zampognari roamed the streets at Christmastime playing bagpipe music, I just wasn't expecting them at that moment, and I could tell by the fuss the baby Jesus was making that he wasn't thrilled either. They showed up out of nowhere and startled me so much that I squawked at the top of my voice and leaped out of Allessandro's arms, flapping my wings as hard as I could. Before I could get far, Alessandro reached out and grabbed me tight around the middle and that egg that I had been trying so hard not to lay, popped right out of me. It sailed through the air and plopped right down in the manger, breaking open on the blanket and splattering egg all over the baby Jesus! I was mortified.

The Presepi was in chaos, those zampognari pipers combined with my outburst scared the sheep so bad they were bleating at the top of their voices. Bruno was squealing and pulling at his rope trying to get away, the missus was crying as she tried to wipe the egg off her baby's face, and the crowd was laughing so hard I saw a few of them wiping away tears. My mister pushed his way through to the front and grabbed Alessandro's arm and told him to bring me home.

At least that's what I thought he said, who could hear anything clearly over the screeching of the zampogna?

When Alessandro got me home, I went and hid in the lantana bush. I was devastated. All I could think about was if this terrible thing that happened was enough to keep me from getting my treats. Was La Befana in the crowd of onlookers? Did she see what I did? Surely she knew it was an accident. She had to know that if that was the real baby Jesus I would never have done such a thing. I just didn't know what to think any more. Being good is a very hard thing to do.

Somehow, I made it through the rest of the Christmas season, but I had a hard time enjoying it. I heard strangers greeting each other with a hearty "Buon Natale" on the streets. I enjoyed seeing the candles through the windows and getting the leftovers from the many delicious dinners my missus made for her family and friends over the holidays. But as January 6th got closer, I got more and more depressed. I was sure that my performance at the Presepi was known to La Befana by now, and she would be giving me a lump of coal instead of a lump of stinkbugs. Stinkbugs are my favorite.

On the morning of January 6th, the sun was just starting to brighten the sky when the door to our coop opened. I opened my eyes halfway, too depressed at La Befana's arrival to get a good look at her. In the semi-darkness she looked an awful lot like Allesandro. I saw her go from nestbox to nestbox, leaving something in each. When she got to the nestbox I was fond of using, I knew she was leaving a lump of coal. If chickens could cry, I would have cried right then in disappointment.

After she left the sky continued to brighten and our rooster welcomed the day the way he always does, with a magnificent crow.

I sat dejectedly on the roost as my chicken friends stretched and hopped down, ready to start their day. It wasn't long before one of them peeked into a nest box and let out a surprised, happy squawk. Everyone else ran over to investigate, and soon they all had beaks full of the wonderful treat that La Befana left for them. I couldn't put it off any longer, I had to go and at least see what a lump of coal looks like. I hopped down and dragged my feet over to the nesting box in the corner where I always laid my eggs. There, in a little basket made of straw, was a lump. I smelled it and it didn't smell like something bad, so I gave it a peck and to my astonishment it was panettone! La Befana left me a large lump of panettone cake complete with cranberries and raisins baked right in!

We were all so busy enjoying our treat that we didn't notice that Alessandro had opened the door and was smiling at all of us. He walked over to me and gave me a couple of pats on my top feathers, laughed and called me his little birichina- his mischievous little girl. That was the Christmas I decided that even though it's fun to believe in someone like La Befana, the real joy is in having friends like Alessandro.

Crowing for Gingerbread, Nuremberg, Germany, Present Day

M y missus makes the best gingerbread. It's something I look forward to every year. This year she's determined to win the competition for making the best lebkuchenhaus in the whole village. A lebkuchenhaus isn't a house for misters and missuses to live in, it's too small. It's a house made of gingerbread and other treats that you can put on your table for people to look at and nibble on. Some people make their lebkuchenhaus look like a real house, some make them look like churches, or castles. I'm secretly hoping that this year, my missus will make hers look like a chicken coop. I think that would be festive and a definite prize winner since I have never heard of anyone creating a chicken coop gingerbread house before. That's a way better idea than a castle. I never knew where people got the idea to turn tasty gingerbread into houses at Christmas time until I heard a story my missus was reading to her children one evening before they went to bed.

My missus read a story from a big book written by the Grimm Brothers about an old missus who built a real sized house out of gingerbread and sweets. The story called this lady a witch. I don't know what that word means, but anyone who lives in a house made of gingerbread and sweets must be wonderful! One day, some lost children found her house in the woods and since they were hungry, they helped themselves and ate pieces of tasty gingerbread off of her house. I suppose some people think they should have asked permission before they started eating the witch's house, but I completely understand why they did it. I wander around all day helping myself to beetles and caterpillars, I never ask them first before I eat them. Well, these two children were named Hansel and Gretel, and the witch invited Hansel in to stay with her. She even let him live in a giant cage so he would be protected from any wild animals that might sneak into the house to attack him in the night. Wasn't that nice of her? She thought he was too skinny so she fed him all the cake and candy he could eat. That sounds like a great life to me! I didn't hear how the story ended because I got distracted by a large grasshopper that went hopping by, so I had to chase it and eat it. But I do still have dreams at night about that wonderful witch and her house made of gingerbread!

Though my missus is a great baker and always does a good job making gingerbread, there's one obstacle she must overcome to win the contest this year- Mrs. Gruber. Mrs. Gruber is our next-door neighbor, and she wins the lebkuchenhaus contest every year. But I predict she won't win this year and the reason I think that is because

I'm going to make sure she doesn't win. I don't like Mrs. Gruber. She's always complaining to my missus about me because I like to crow. All roosters like to crow, that's just who we are. She has a rooster who likes to crow too, I hear him all the time. Of course, he isn't as good a rooster as I am because I never hear him crowing in the middle of the night like I do. Crowing is my job, and I take it very seriously. If I wake up in the middle of the night, I remember what I was born to do and I do it. She says it wakes her up when I'm crowing at three o'clock in the morning, but I think she's just jealous because her rooster isn't as hard a worker as I am and doesn't crow at night like I do. I've actually heard her suggest to my missus that she get rid of me because of all my crowing! That doesn't worry me, my missus isn't a dummy, she knows a good rooster when she hears one and I'm definitely here to stay. Still, I think Mrs. Gruber needs to be taught a lesson.

My plan is to eat Mrs. Gruber's gingerbread so she won't be able to make it into a lebkuchenhaus. This shouldn't be a problem since I'm a good eater. I know she likes to put her gingerbread out on her windowsill to cool as soon as it comes out of the oven. That's when I'll pounce and knock it out of the windowsill onto the dirt where I can help myself. Chickens don't mind a little dirt in our food, it helps our digestion.

Sure enough, the next morning I could smell the delicious aroma of gingerbread coming from Mrs. Gruber's kitchen. I spent a lot of time lurking in her backyard so I would be ready for my mission as soon as she opened her window. The only problem I encountered was that now, of all days, her rooster decided to start acting like a rooster, he actually bristled up when he saw me. I'm not friends with that rooster because he's a scaredy cat and runs away whenever he sees me, but for some reason, today it looks like he's decided to protect his missus's gingerbread and wants to chase me out of his yard. Well, roosters don't back down from a fight and I wasn't about to let him chase me away so, I did what anyone would do, I bristled up at him and we stared at each other, daring the other one to start the fight. Not even the sound of Mrs. Gruber's windowsill opening could distract me from the impending battle. It was when I glanced at the windowsill that my neighbor made his move. He leaped at me and tried to spur me with his sharp spurs, but I was too quick. We silently continued leaping at each other and bristling our feathers. I don't think either one of us drew blood, our hearts simply weren't in it, how could we concentrate with that gingerbread sitting on a windowsill mere feet away?

I don't know if I purposely inched closer to the windowsill as we were lunging at each other, but before I knew it, we were directly under the tasty gingerbread cooling in the winter afternoon air. We both paused for a moment, maybe because we were tired from jumping around and knew a snack would give us the energy to fight to the finish. That's when I jumped up and the top of my head hit the edge of the pan flipping the gingerbread off the windowsill and onto the ground below. My opponent seemed shocked to see his missus's prized gingerbread cracked into pieces in the dirt, I'm sure he didn't know what to do. So, I was a good neighbor and showed him that the only thing to do was take a bite.

It didn't take long before the hens of both our flocks noticed that we were done fighting and on to more important things, so they joined us. In a few minutes all of us finished off that delicious gingerbread, leaving only a few crumbs behind for the ants. We were smart enough to know that we needed to scatter before the missus saw us and figured out what happened. I was all the way on the other side of our house taking a dust bath when I heard Mrs. Gruber scream when she saw the empty pan in the dirt outside the window.

My missus won the lebkuchenhaus contest that year, as I knew she would. She didn't make a chicken coop like I was hoping, but I'm sure I'll find a way to suggest that to her for next year. And as for the rooster next door, we're best friends now. We walk around together, each regulating his own flock. We're such good friends we've become fond of communicating with each other, whenever we're apart and he hears me crow, he crows in return. Chickens don't smile, but I would have smiled last night at three o'clock in the morning when I crowed and a moment later, heard him crow in his own coop in return. Take that, Mrs. Gruber.

Carpy, the Bathtub Fish, Turnov, Czech Republic, Present Day

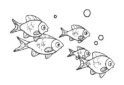

T he family has definitely taken things too far this time. I know
they have a lot of children and the children like pets, so I think
I've been very understanding of all the pets that have come to live in
the house while I live in a smelly chicken coop. I watch all day as the
dog and the cat run in and out whenever they want. I'm not envious
of them because they were already here when I hatched. There's a
pecking order and the dog and the cat are above me, and I can respect
that. But the others, well, that's a different story.

First there was the lizard. I was jealous the day Antonin caught
him in the yard and put him in a cardboard box and brought him
into the house. I know that lizard personally, he was always running
around the front yard and just as I got close enough to snap him up he
would run and hide under a rock. I think he was mocking me. I should

have eaten him while I had the chance. Now he lives in comfort and warmth in Antonin's bedroom.

Then, I held my tongue when the youngest girl, Elena, came home a few days ago with her class pet in a large cage. She said it was her job to take care of it during the Christmas holidays. That creature looked an awful lot like a mouse, but fluffier. I hate mice. They get in our chicken coop and eat our food. Now the mouse is living in the house and from what I've seen by looking through the window into Elena's bedroom, all it does is run on a wheel all day long. Where does it think it's going? How dumb can you be! But that mouse and the lizard are living in luxury in the family home while I'm out here scratching around in the snow in search of frozen caterpillars.

If all that wasn't enough, this morning I saw the mister get out of his car and carry a plastic bag full of water and an enormous fish into the house. They named that fish "Carpy" and now he's living his best fish life in the family bathtub. I can't believe it! I've always disapproved of bathtubs because I think getting clean using water is misguided. Chickens take a nice dust bath and by the time we've shaken all that dirt off of us we are sparkling clean. Getting clean with water is an odd idea, but it's how the family does it, only now, since their bathtub is occupied by Carpy, they'll all be dirty on Christmas day because they can't take a bath with that fish. Honestly, something has to be done.

So now it's the day before Christmas Eve and even the smell of boiling potatoes isn't cheering me up. Usually, that's one of my favorite smells. My missus is making a giant bowl of potato salad for the Christmas Eve dinner, she does it every year. Probably this year she'll toss a scoop of her delicious potato salad into the bathtub so

Carpy can have a festive meal. But I promised myself I wouldn't think of him any more since thoughts of him ruin my Christmas spirit.

Right now my mister is out on the garden shed making the walnut boats. He cracks walnuts in half and empties the shells out then fills them with candle wax to make tiny floating candles that the family will float in a pail of water. Depending on which way the candles float the family will get some clues about how their lives will go in the coming year. If the boats sink that's not a good sign. That's when they'll get out the apples. They slice an apple in half and if they see a star in the pattern of the seeds that means their lives will be great! If they see a cross in the pattern, that means they'll die. Ever since I learned how that works I steer clear of apples. It's a shame because apples sure are tasty.

After they float some walnut candles and slice the apples all the missusses will take off their shoes and throw them at the door. If the shoe lands facing the door it means she will get married in the coming year. I don't know why they all want to get married so badly, it seems like a lot of trouble to me.

You may be wondering how I know so much about the family traditions at Christmas time, I know because I was hatched in an incubator in the laundry room a couple of weeks before Christmas last year. I spent my first month of life living with my brothers and sisters in a cage on top of the washing machine. I got to see the wonders of Christmas first hand, and I got to feel how nice it is to live in a warm house filled with love and laughter. Now the lizard, the fluffy mouse, and Carpy the bathtub fish get to enjoy all that and I get exactly- nothing.

I woke up Christmas Eve morning in a grumpy mood. Even the smell of my missus's homemade Trdelník cake couldn't make me feel better, I was bitter and refused to be grateful for what I had because all I could do was focus on what I didn't have. I heard the children running around the yard talking excitedly about what gifts they thought the baby Jesus would bring them that night while they were eating dinner. It confuses me to think about a baby being able to carry gifts into the house since all the babies I've ever seen are pretty helpless, but maybe I don't know everything there is to know about everything. While I was thinking about all this I heard my missus call the children to come into the house and while they ran in the front door I saw my mister sneak out the back door and what he was carrying shocked the feathers off of me.

I followed my mister out to the garden shed. I stood in the doorway and watched as my mister laid Carpy down on his workbench. Carpy seemed to be in a good mood, he was wiggling and flapping his fins around like he was swimming, and he wasn't even in any water. He was probably looking forward to Christmas with the family. But then my mister grabbed a cleaver and chopped Carpy's head off. That was an unexpected development for me, and probably for Carpy too. Long story short, Carpy lost his scales and his insides right there in the garden shed. As the grandparents and aunts, uncles, and cousins started to arrive, my mister scooped up a couple of poor Carpy's scales and put them in his wallet for good luck, then carried what was left of Carpy back into the house through the back door. I wonder what my mister will tell the children when they ask why Carpy isn't swimming around the bathtub any more, maybe he'll tell them that Carpy went to live in a big pond on a farm out in the country where he'll have plenty of room to swim and lots of other fish friends to play with. I don't know what explanation he'll give the children, all I know is it wasn't long before we could smell the aroma of fried fish coming from the kitchen.

If I was that lizard or that fluffy mouse I would be getting nervous right about then.

I learned a lesson that night. Basically, whatever bad things were going on in my life, at least I wasn't Carpy. I learned that Christmas should be a time of gratitude. I realized that I was grateful for the family and my chicken friends. I was also grateful for the love and joy I felt at Christmas. But mostly I was grateful for good food. Later that evening my missus brought us the table scraps for our good night snack, and I can honestly say, Carpy was delicious.

A Boxing Day Surprise, Manitoba, Canada, Present Day

M ost folks are excited because today is Christmas Day, but not me, I'm saving my excitement for tomorrow- tomorrow is Boxing Day! I know all about Boxing Day. My mister's son Horace did a report on it for school a few weeks ago and I overheard him reading it to his parents. Apparently, in the olden days Boxing Day was a day to recognize and give gifts to everyone who has served you during the year. You're supposed to get a giant box and fill it with treats for those who have worked hard for you. That got me thinking, who works harder than chickens? I've probably laid about a thousand eggs this year, that's a lot of work. Of course that's just an estimate, I don't really know how to count, and I don't know how many days there are in a year, but a thousand sounds about right. That means I should get a thousand treats in my Boxing Day box! Who needs Santa Claus when you have Boxing Day to look forward to?

Boxing Day seems to mean something different for everyone. For my missus it means a long hard day of backbreaking work. On Boxing Day my missus gets up when it's still dark outside and goes out for a long, grueling day of shopping. It doesn't seem fair that she has to work on Boxing Day, but for some reason she seems excited to get up early and get to town for all the bargains. I don't know what bargains are, but it must be important because I heard her talking about how she wants to be there before the doors open. How is she going to get bargains if she can't even get in the door? It's a mystery. I hope her mister and her children make sure and have a box of treats waiting for her when she gets home since she's such a hard worker.

My mister and his friends spend Boxing Day playing hockey in the house. I didn't know there was ice inside the house, I assumed it was like our chicken coop and had a dirt floor. It also doesn't seem big enough to be playing hockey in there but of course I'm not tall enough to see in the windows and know how much room there is. I know all about hockey because we have a pond here on our property where the little boys, Horace and Jimmy, like to practice. I don't play hockey myself because I don't have skates. I'm not sure why everyone plays hockey in the house on Boxing Day, but I know they do because I can hear them halfway across the yard yelling "hustle" and "start the clock." And apparently, some guy named "Idiot" always comes to play hockey at our house because I can hear my mister yelling his name all the time.

So, for now I just have to get through Christmas Day and get some good rest so I can wake up early and collect my Boxing Day box. Ever since I heard about Boxing Day, I've been dreaming about what will be in my box. One of my favorite Christmas time treats is called a tourtière. A tourtière is a meat pie with a very flaky crust. Last year I got one bite of it in the supper scraps and it was the best thing I ever tasted. Since this treat will be special just for my Boxing Day box, I'm hoping my missus chooses chopped grasshoppers for the filling. For dessert I would love to have a Buche de Noël. That's a Christmas cake shaped like a log. Logs are one of my favorite places to find lunch. You can get termites, spiders, and even centipedes when you're scratching around an old, fallen log. I hope the Buche de Noël my missus makes for me has termites baked right in!

While I was thinking about my box, I spent some time scratching near the pond watching Jimmy and Horace practicing their hockey skills out on the frozen water. They got new skates from Santa Claus, so I guess they were trying to make sure they fit well so they will be ready for the big game tomorrow. Poor Jimmy and Horace, they have to settle for Santa and won't be getting a Boxing Day box like me because they don't lay eggs.

As I was watching them, I heard a sharp crack, and down they went into the freezing cold water. Our pond isn't deep, I've seen the boys wade completely across it in the summertime and the water only reaches up to their chests. But it's not summer and they must be cold. When they fell in it startled me so much, I let out a screech and started fussing. Chickens are easily startled and we're always on the lookout for predators so whenever something unexpected happens we start to fuss. Well, my fussing brought the missus to the window and then I heard her scream out my mister's name. Well, they both came running out of the house along with the grandparents and aunts and uncles and everyone else who had been enjoying the Christmas afternoon. The whole herd of them went running full speed towards the water. By then, the boys had hauled themselves out and were laying on the ice shivering and crying. My mister and an uncle carried them back indoors and I'm sure they spent some time getting them warmed up.

Since the excitement was over and the sun was starting to fade, I joined the other hens in the hen house. I thought it would be hard to fall asleep because I was excited for the morning and the Boxing Day box, but I must have fallen asleep quickly because before I even knew it, it was morning.

My mister let us out of the coop and tossed us some grain just like he does every morning. In fact, there was nothing special going on at all, did he forget about me and the thousands of eggs I had laid this past year? I was disappointed, but decided to peck at the grain before my colleagues got it all. As I was pecking with my back turned, my mister scooped me up and took me back into the coop and shut the door. At first, I thought I was in trouble, but then he set me down in a nesting box and took a small plastic container from his coat pocket. When he took the lid off, I could see it was a whole piece of tourtière, and it was just for me!

As I ate my meat pie all by myself my mister started rambling about what a good hen I was for saving his sons from something called a hypothermia. We have lots of predators around our farm, but I'd never heard of a hypothermia and I wondered if it was anything like a hawk. But my meat pie was so delicious that I decided to think of all that later and concentrate on eating. As he kept talking, I felt a little guilty that he thought I made the fuss to let him know the boys had fallen in and needed help, when really, I was just startled and reacted by fussing. Maybe if he knew I didn't do it to save the boys he would take my tourtière away, and I couldn't let that happen, so I kept eating.

That afternoon, as everyone was in the house yelling and playing hockey, I perched on a fencepost and dozed in the afternoon sun. My tummy was full of tourtière and even though I didn't think that pie was made of chopped grasshoppers, it was definitely the best thing I've ever eaten. I thought to myself that I would try and lay five thousand eggs this coming year so I could have even more pie next Boxing Day. As I dozed off, I heard everyone in the house yelling at that mister named "Idiot" and I thought to myself that this was the best Boxing Day ever.

The Yule Lads and Their Cat, Reykjavik, Iceland, Present Day

I t's almost Christmas and that concerns me because I haven't been very bad yet. I know most folks this time of the year are trying to be good because they think Santa will bring them treats for being good. Well, here in Iceland, we have something much better than Santa, we have the thirteen Yule Lads! The Yule Lads are trolls who live in the mountains. They come down from the mountains one at a time the thirteen days before Christmas and play pranks around town. If you're a child and you've been good, you can leave a shoe on your windowsill and the Yule Lads will leave a treat in your shoe every night for thirteen nights. But if you're bad they leave a potato in your shoe instead. That's why I have to be bad. I'm not fond of sweets but potatoes are a different story. Potatoes are a fabulous thing because there are so many kinds of potatoes. Some potatoes are called baked potatoes, some are called boiled potatoes, and some are called fried potatoes. There are also soup potatoes and potato pancakes. Potatoes are so much better than cookies and candy! I must be very badly behaved so a Yule Lad will bring me my favorite potato- mashed potato. This kind of potato grows into a giant glob of mush that tastes like the best thing in the whole world. I'm not a good counter so I'm not sure how many days are left until Christmas, all I know is I better get to being bad soon so I don't miss out.

Being bad is not really a hard thing to do, I'm just not sure how bad I have to be to show the Yule Lads that I deserve a mashed potato. Yesterday I stole a beetle right out of another hen's mouth, I wonder if that's bad enough? Then I laid an egg and promptly turned around and pecked it open and ate it, that was extra bad! Then I hopped up and pecked my missus's hand when she was unlatching the gate. She tried to swat me, but I was too quick for her and ran away fast. After all that bad behavior I expected a mashed potato to be waiting for me this morning, but I was disappointed.

I guess I just haven't been bad enough. I didn't want it to come to this, but I know what I have to do to get the attention of the Yule Lads. I'm going to have to get rid of their cat.

Oh, I know all about their cat. One of my favorite pastimes is to scratch around outside the window of our house so I can hear my missus read stories to her children. Sometimes I jump up to a low branch on a nearby tree so I can see the pictures in the books. That's how I know the Yule Lads have a cat. The Yule Cat is a creature that comes down from the hills to gobble up bad children (and probably bad chickens too) at Christmas time. It doesn't sound like a very light and happy Christmas story if you ask me. According to the tales, this cat doesn't like it if you don't wear the new clothes you got for

Christmas. If it catches you without your new socks or new sweater on, it goes after you. Why does the cat care about your new clothes? Who knows? No one knows what goes on in the mind of a cat.

After I heard that story, I spent many sleepless nights worried about the Yule Cat catching me without my clothes on, which is not hard to do because I never wear clothes. It was stressful always looking around in all directions to make sure the Yule Cat wasn't lurking behind a tree waiting to gobble me up. Imagine my surprise when one day, my mister actually brought the Yule Cat home to live with us! He got out of the car with a small, furry creature in his arms. His daughters ran out of the house and instead of being horrified to find that their own father brought that monstrous creature home, they were happy to have it!

I've seen pictures of the Yule Cat in the story books the missus reads to the girls. I thought it would be enormous, but it's a lot smaller than it looks in the books. It doesn't look big enough to gobble up a child, but maybe it could gobble up a medium sized chicken, that's part of why I have to get rid of it. I'm a medium sized chicken.

The Yule Cat spends its days wandering around our farm and pretending to be a sweet, loving creature, not the bloodthirsty monster I know it really is. One time I saw that cat rubbing up against one of the little girl's legs and I was worried because she didn't have any socks on, and I didn't want her to get gobbled up. But it wasn't Christmas time when that happened, maybe the Yule Cat only gets vicious the thirteen days before Christmas.

So, here's my plan. My mister is making some poison in the shed behind the house. I know it's poison because it smells horrible. My mister said he was making fermented skate, which is a type of fish, and they were all going to eat it for dinner the day before Christmas Eve. But I think he must be joking, no one would eat something that smells so disgusting! I plan on luring the Yule Cat into the shed and then I'm going to jump up and knock that container of fishy poison all over the cat and that will be the end of him. Surely that will be a bad enough deed to get me my mashed potato!

I didn't have much of a problem getting the cat to chase me into the shed. The Yule Cat is very playful, I think he pretends to play when really he's just trying to trick us all into thinking he's harmless. When I saw him in the yard I ran over and hopped around in front of him to get his attention, then I chased him a bit. He scooted under a bench and crouched down, I knew that meant he would chase me when I ran by. That's how I got him into the shed. We were running fast and the Yule Cat didn't have time to slow down when I suddenly leaped up, and flapped my wings so I could land up on the table where the container with fermenting skate fish poison was sitting. Icelandic chickens are great flyers, plus we're very strong because we're descendants of the Vikings. Everyone knows that no chickens in the world were stronger, or better in battle than Viking chickens.

Maybe it was because my mind was preoccupied with the mashed potato I was hoping to earn that I didn't aim as well as I should have. My wing caught the edge of the container, it flipped over and that rotting, smelly, fermented fish splashed   all over me AND the Yule Cat! We both ran as fast as we could out of the shed, but the smell followed us. I watched the Yule Cat rolling on the dirt, desperate to get the smell off of him. I plopped down and used my wings to flip dirt all over me. A dust bath usually works to make me feel clean and happy, but this time it just made that fermented fish juice into a thick mud that stuck to my feathers. Now the Yule Cat and I were both stinky.

That was a hard Christmas for me, I didn't mind when everyone laughed at us. I did mind when my mister got the garden hose and cornered me by the side of the coop and sprayed me down. I noticed my missus took out a wash tub and gave the Yule Cat a bath on the back porch, but alas, it didn't work for either of us. We both stayed stinky for a long time.

That night I slept by myself high up in a tree. I knew no one would want me in the coop since I smelled so bad. My only consolation was I noticed that the Yule Cat had to sleep out on the porch too, at least he wouldn't be gobbling up the children in the night for not wearing their socks. I tried to stay awake to see if a Yule Lad was wandering about looking for someone who might deserve a mashed potato, but I was so exhausted from the activities of the day that I fell asleep, in spite of the smell.

When I woke up Christmas Eve morning I looked down and was surprised to see my missus standing at the bottom of the tree looking up at me. I didn't understand everything she said, but she was yammering on and on about how she wanted to thank me for dumping out the fermented fish because she really didn't want to eat it or have it stink up her house. That made sense to me, I didn't want her to eat poison either. That's when I noticed she had a small plate in her hand. She called to me and dumped out at the base of the tree something that looked an awful lot like a mashed potato. I promptly flew down and investigated, it *was* a mashed potato! The best thing was that since everyone else was locked in the coop, I didn't have to share that mashed potato with anyone- well, almost anyone. I guess I didn't really mind all that much when the Yule Cat sprinted over and timidly approached my feast. I scooted over a bit and shared with him, after all, it was my fault he was stinky and had to sleep on the porch. I wouldn't say we became friends after that, I still watched him closely to make sure he wasn't thinking about eating the children, but I had to admit, it's because of him I got the best Christmas treat ever—a mashed potato all for me.

Saint Nicholas and his Bag of Rocks, Myra, Asia Minor AD 280

My missus is sitting out under a tree with HIM again. That mister comes around here all the time and once, when no one was looking, I saw him holding her hand! I don't know why that's necessary, I would hold her hand if she wanted me to, except I don't have hands...

My missus has two sisters, and we all live here with her father. It's a good life but we have a problem, the father says that the girls must get married and move away but he doesn't have any money to pay the dowry to the misters who want to marry them. That's fine with me, I don't want the girls to move away, especially the youngest girl, my missus. She always picks me up and takes me for little walks with her. She tells me all her problems and I'm a good listener, even though I don't understand all the things she says. Sometimes she saves me a crust of bread from her supper and that means a lot to me because I know the family doesn't have a lot to eat, also, I really like bread. So, I'm going to do my best to make sure she doesn't leave me, no matter how much she seems to like holding hands with that mister when he comes for a visit.

Something strange happened one night, and I don't know what to think about it. We roost in a tree right next to the family home and normally, I'm a hard sleeper. But for some reason, I woke up in the night and saw someone lurking by the window. I don't like lurkers, that's what that hand-holding mister does- he lurks around our house until he can catch my missus when her father can't see him. At first, I thought it WAS that mister peeping in the window, trying to find a way to hold my missus's hand while she was sleeping, but the lurker was too tall to be the hand-holding mister. Still, misters shouldn't be hanging around our house in the middle of the night spying on the girls while they sleep, even I know that's not proper.

I was just about to doze off when suddenly, he took a bag out of his pocket and tossed it in the window. I could tell it was heavy because it made a loud thump when it landed. It was probably full of rocks! He was throwing rocks at the family while they slept! I was just about to jump out of the tree so I could deal with him, but he crept away after he threw the rocks. I know I should have followed him, but I was tired, so I went back to sleep.

I almost forgot about the incident until a couple of days later I noticed that the oldest of the daughters was gone. I don't know where she went. I thought that maybe when the lurker threw the bag of rocks in the window, he hit her in the head and she died! I was pretty upset about it until later in the week when the daughter came back for a visit, and she had a mister with her. She looked happy, so I guess she finally married her mister after all. Chickens aren't good at analyzing cause and effect situations, so, at the time, I didn't make a connection between the bag of rocks and the marriage, it took another nighttime visit for me to start seeing what was really going on.

The moon was full so I could see the lurker a little better when he showed up at our window the second time. I couldn't be sure, but he kind of looked a little like this man Nicholas, who lived in our village. Nicholas worked at the church and everyone in town loved him, they said he was such a good and kind person he would probably become a saint someday. Of course, they didn't know that Nicholas was fond of stalking around at night throwing rocks at sleeping girls' heads. I wasn't about to let him get away with it this time. As he approached the window, I could see him grab the bag from his pocket and reach his arm up to throw. Since the moon was so bright I could see directly into the house from my perch in the tree and I saw the girls sleeping on their mats by the fire. They looked so peaceful, they didn't know that one of them was about to get bonked on the head with a bag of rocks! Not on my watch! Just as Nicholas was about to toss the bag, I let out a loud squawk. He was so startled it threw his aim off and I watched as that bag sailed through the air and landed straight into one of the stockings that were hung by the fire to dry. At least it didn't hit anybody in the head. That Nicholas fellow took off running down the street, I hoped he had learned his lesson this time and wouldn't be back for any more lurking.

I was wrong. The second oldest daughter disappeared much like the first, I assumed she had headed off to get married too, I didn't see it happen, I can't watch the house all day, I have to scratch around and hunt up beetles and grasshoppers so I will have the strength to keep watch over the last remaining daughter- my missus. By now I had figured out that there was a connection between the rock-throwing and my missuses leaving home. I wasn't about to lose my favorite missus. If it meant staying up all night, I would do what I had to do, but I knew I had to have a plan.

I started sleeping under an oleander bush next to the window so I could do more than just squawk when Nicholas arrived. I'm not good at counting so I don't know how many days passed before he showed up again, I just know that he almost stepped on my toe with his sandal when he came to throw rocks at my favorite missus's head. I was still half asleep, but my instincts kicked in and that, combined with my love for my missus, gave me the strength to reach out and bite him as hard as I could. Chickens don't have teeth, but our beaks are strong and there was no way I was going to let him attack my missus.

When I struck, he let out a high-pitched yelp, which was not very saintly if you ask me. But more importantly, he was so startled he dropped his bag of rocks on the ground and the bag opened up spilling its contents on the dirt. Even in the semi-darkness I could see that it wasn't rocks in that bag, it was gold coins! Nicholas had been throwing money into the house at night, enough money to pay the dowries for the girls so they could go off and hold hands with their misters all they wanted!

By now, the father and my missus were awake and were looking out the window at us. I don't know what they talked about with Nicholas because I was busy fussing and making sure they knew that I was the one who had saved them, but since everyone started crying and giving window hugs, I guess they weren't mad at Nicholas for trying to kill them with bags of heavy gold.

A few days later I was scratching around in front of the house when my missus's mister arrived with a bouquet of flowers and an extra horse. My missus came out of the house dressed in her best skirt, she was blushing and had tears in her eyes. I saw her father hand him that bag of gold he got from Nicholas, then she hugged him and let that mister help her up on his extra horse and off they went.

After that I was so depressed I could hardly eat. When our rooster discovered an old log crawling with juicy termites, I ran over with everyone else and fought to get the fattest ones, but my heart just wasn't in it. I missed her and I couldn't help hating Nicholas for his part in taking her away from me.

The story of the gold in the stocking spread around our village quickly and folks were always stopping by to chat with father about it. They all praised Nicholas for his generosity and for his creativity in leaving the gold in the stocking. Humph, that only happened because of me, but no one said anything nice about me. That made me hate Nicholas even more. Then, one morning, when the sun was barely up and I was still asleep in the tree, I was shocked when Nicholas himself lifted me down out of the tree and carried me away.

I thought he was certainly going to punish me for biting him like I did, maybe he would hit me in the head with rocks until I died. But to my amazement, that's not what happened at all. After a short walk to the other side of the village he carried me up a pretty path lined with flowers to a small, neat house with blue curtains. Before we even got to the door my missus opened it and ran down the path to meet us. I could see joy in her eyes, not because she saw Nicholas, but because she saw me. She lifted me out of his arms and covered me in kisses. It was the happiest day of my life. She said I was to live with her and her mister now and I could go with her when she went for visits to her father. She took a large crust of bread out of her pocket and gave it to me right there in front of Nicholas. She didn't give him any bread at all.

All that I've said is a true story. I'm an old hen now and my missus has a baby that she brings with her to sit on the grass on a blanket. I know she loves her baby, but she loves me more because she always brings me bread and I have never once seen her give a crust of bread to the baby. Sometimes Nicholas stops by for a visit, and I don't hate him anymore. I know his good deeds have made my missus, and me, happy. He's taught me that it's a good thing to give gifts to others, maybe someday there will be a special day of the year when everyone gives gifts to those they love.

I guess it would be fine with me if someday, they make Nicholas a saint. I wonder if they let chickens become saints? Who knows, maybe I'll become a saint too, after all, the gold in the stocking was my idea...

The Arrival of Sinterklaas, Bergen op Zoom, Netherlands, Present Day

C hickens don't wear shoes. That's a problem for me because I can tell that St. Nicholas Day is almost here. That means Sinterklaas will be arriving any day now and if I don't have any shoes how will Sinterklaas leave me any treats? Sinterklaas is an old man with white hair. He wears a red robe and cape and carries a giant red book that has the names of all the children who have behaved badly in the last year. I'm not worried about my name being in that book since I don't have a name. I used to be sad about that, but now I know it's a good thing because I can get into trouble whenever I want without worrying about my name being written in that book.

Sinterklaas likes to leave his treats in shoes and since I like treats, I will have to find a way to fix the problem of my lack of shoes. In the meantime, I'm on the lookout for him. I know he always arrives on a boat from far away Spain. Once he gets here, he will travel the streets of our town greeting everyone, and at night, if you leave your shoes out, Sinterklaas will fill them with treats. I was just newly hatched last year when Sinterklaas got to town, and no one bothered to tell me about the shoes. Chickens love treats and it was torture for me to see all the good things the children got last year. Their wooden shoes were filled with marzipan and mandarin oranges, and each child had a piece of chocolate made in the shape of the first letter of their name. Each shoe even had some of my favorite cookies in them- Kruidnootjes. Kruidnootjes are perfect for me because they're small and I can easily pick one up and run away with it before my chicken friends can grab it from me. The chicken word is brutal- even at Christmastime we steal treats from one another. I can just taste the Kruidnootjes now! I hope Sinterklaas can also fit some crickets and beetles in my shoe along with the Kruidnootjes. If I had a shoe filled with Kruidnootjes, crickets, and beetles I would be the happiest chicken on the planet! But what to do about the shoes?

My first idea was to use a walnut shell for a shoe because they're hard like our wooden Dutch shoes and I didn't think Sinterklaas would notice that they weren't real shoes. I was able to get about half of one of my toes in the shell, but the shell was too wide and wouldn't stay on my toe. Then I decided to try acorn shells. Those worked well because one of them could fit nicely on a toe. I was able to find enough shells for all my toes but then I had a problem scratching around with those shells on. Also walking was a bit hard. Also, the other hens made fun of me. It's probably for the best that I had to give up on that idea because acorn shells are very small, so small that a Kruidnootjes probably wouldn't even fit. I'm not even sure a decent size beetle would fit in one. My last idea was to use a tulip flower. Since this is Holland there are always plenty of tulips around, tulips are our thing. I found a very pretty pink tulip and most of my foot would actually fit inside it, but it wasn't very sturdy and fell apart the minute I tried to walk. Sigh. I had to come up with a better idea.

Since I don't have a name and therefore am not in danger of having my name written in Sinterklaas's big red book of naughty chickens, I decided the only thing left to do would be to steal a shoe. I had to choose carefully because I wasn't strong enough to drag a full-grown person's shoe over to the coop, but I didn't want a baby shoe because it wouldn't have room for lots of treats. I ended up deciding on our neighbor's youngest child's shoe. She was little, but not too little, and her shoe had a small crack on the heel so I could fit the bottom of my beak in the crack and get a good hold on it. Best of all, that child often left her shoes outside when she kicked them off to play, so I knew the chances were high that I could find one of her shoes. I waited until the evening, when most of the hens were already in the coop, before I snuck over and dragged that little shoe over and hid it in some bushes on the side of our coop. Stealing is a terrible thing and I thought I would have trouble sleeping after my crime, but I slept surprisingly well since I was so excited to be ready for Sinterklaas's arrival.

I didn't have to wait long, a few days later I could hear excitement coming from all over town. Large groups of people headed down to the water to welcome Sinterklass as he came in on his boat. I knew I didn't have to go down to the water because he would soon be parading down the street right in front of our house. Some of the other hens joined me, we were excited because Sinterklaas's helpers often threw candy out into the crowd, and everyone likes a good piece of candy.

As people began to line the streets I wandered up near the front, desperate to make eye contact with Sinterklaas when he arrived so he could see into my heart and know how worthy I was of a shoe full of treats. Finally, I could see him coming down the street, riding majestically on his white horse! And that's when I noticed that he wasn't alone. My heart sank. How could I have forgotten? Zwart Piet! I saw him running around the street with that huge jute bag, ready to stuff the bad children in the bag and take them back to Spain with him. Was it possible that he knew I stole the shoe? Even though I didn't have a name, could my description be written in that big red book? I didn't want to go to Spain! Who knows what goes on in Spain? Maybe they treat chickens badly in Spain, I'd heard of places that actually eat chickens, maybe Spain was one of those places! I couldn't risk it, I had to get off the street and run away and hide, but the people were packed in so tightly behind me that there was no way through. The only way would be to sprint out into the street and run down in front of the crowd until I found a break in the people to scoot through.

As I pushed my way through the crowd and out onto the street I noticed a commotion behind me, Zwart Piet spotted me! He laughed loudly and started to chase me, swinging that jute bag as he went. I was so terrified I zig-zagged all over the street, trying to get on the other side of the crowd so I could run for the safety of my coop, but the people were packed in too thickly, there was no path through! The crowd roared with laughter as he chased me forward and backwards and side to side, my neck stretched out, my feet flying.

Just when I was almost completely out of energy and unable to keep going, I skidded right into someone standing in the middle of the street. I felt hands grasp me around the middle and I expected the darkness of that jute bag to envelope me at any moment. But instead, I was lifted up and held gently, my body safe in kind arms against a warm chest. I barely had the strength to lift my head, but when I did, it wasn't Piet that I saw, it was Sinterklaas himself! He smiled at me, then he reached a hand in his pocket and pulled out a Kruidnootjes, just for me! Though I was weak from the chase, I couldn't help but start to peck on that tasty cookie he held in the palm of his hand. I heard the crowd around me clap and call out Sinterklaas's name, but I was enjoying my Kruidnootjes so much that I hardly noticed when my mister came out of the crowd to claim me. Sinterklaas handed me gently to him along with a whole bag of Kruidnootjes and instructions that those cookies were to be shared with all my chicken friends.

That afternoon, as we spread out in our yard, happily pecking at enough Kruidnootjes to fill all our tummies with happiness, I thought of Sinterklaas and his kindness. I knew that later in the afternoon I would have to pull that shoe out of the bushes and return it to the child I stole it from. I had deserved to be tossed into Piet's jute bag and taken away to a life far from home, but because of kindness, Sinterklaas made sure I wouldn't get what I deserved. Maybe kindness is the key, maybe kindness is what makes this time of the year so special.

Roosters, Alpacas, and Llamas- Oh my! Cusco, Peru, Present Day

I 'm excited because I'm going on vacation. I've never been on vacation before. A hen I know went on vacation for three weeks and when she came back, she had eleven chicks with her, I hope that doesn't happen to me. I'm still young and I don't want to be tied down with chicks to take care of. Of course, I won't be gone more than a day or two, maybe that isn't long enough for a bunch of chicks to find me and want to be with me. Plus, I'm a rooster and from what I've seen, roosters don't seem to be wandering around with chicks all that much.

I have to get to town because tomorrow is Christmas Eve and I don't want to be late for the Misa de Gallo. The Misa de Gallo is the Rooster Mass. A Mass is a church service and since I've never been to church before, I'm excited for the opportunity. To think that in town they have a special Christmas Eve church service that's just for roosters!

I suppose I could walk down the hill to get to town, but it's a long walk and I want to keep my energy up so I can explore the town before church. So, I'm going to hide in my missus's bolsa that she always straps to Panchito when they walk down every morning for their job. My missus works as an alpaca lady and Panchito works as an alpaca. Every day they go into town and let people take pictures of them in their colorful clothing. I love my missus, I don't love Panchito. Panchito is very spoiled. My missus washes him, so his fur is always clean and fluffy. She puts girly bows in his hair, which he doesn't seem to mind. She feeds him the best food and sings songs to him while he's eating. I don't know what's so special about Panchito that people want to take pictures with him. I wish my missus would take me to town, I bet she would earn twice as much letting people take pictures of me since I'm a very handsome rooster. I'm red with black tail feathers and when the sun strikes my feathers they shine and look almost blue and green. Panchito is gray. How boring.

It was a little tricky hiding in my missus's bolsa since I had to wait until she had it secured around Panchito's neck. Then I had to jump in when she wasn't looking. I'm still young so I'm not very big and not very heavy, but wouldn't you know it, Panchito protested anyway. I think he was just mad because he knows I'm better looking than him and his job as a fancy alpaca picture model is in danger.

It didn't take long to get to town- once my missus turned her back to talk to a friend I hopped out and raced around the corner. I'm a country rooster so being in town was quite a shock for me, there were people everywhere. Most were dressed in the colorful clothing of the region, but there were also plenty of people who must be tourists, I can tell because their clothing is colorless and dull.

Once I got around the corner and into the square, I was overwhelmed with how festive everything was. They call this place the Plaza de Armas and it was filled with people and vendors and a large nativity scene near the church. I was so busy looking at everything that I almost got stepped on by a llama who was roaming around with his missus looking for a tourist who needed a picture. Llamas are like alpacas but bigger.

I decided to hightail it out of the plaza because if I got squashed by a llama, I would definitely have to miss the Rooster Mass and there was no way I was going to miss that. Once I turned down a street into a quieter section of town, I heard a group of children laughing, so I decided to see what was going on.

Some roosters are mean to children and like to chase them around, but I'm not like that. Children often have cookies or other treats in their pockets and if I walk behind them, sometimes they drop their treats and that's an opportunity I can't pass up. I followed the sound and found a large courtyard filled with children and their mamas. Everyone was laughing and singing and eating. Since they were drinking cups of what I assumed was hot chocolate, I knew I had arrived at a chocolatada. I had heard about these events, sometimes they were just an opportunity for groups of friends to gather together and share stories and drink hot chocolate, sometimes they were larger events where less fortunate children could come and get a treat and a present. I don't know why here in Peru we like to drink hot chocolate at Christmas when this time of the year is our summertime and it's not very chilly, but people sure do love their hot chocolate.

I decided to stay and see if someone would throw a cookie at me, it was getting late in the afternoon and I hadn't eaten since breakfast.

When my tummy was finally full of cookies, I hopped up on a low wall in a quiet place to take a little nap. I knew the Rooster Mass would be later that night and I needed some rest. I don't know how long I was asleep, but I was rudely awakened by a loud bellow and the hot breath of that very same llama that almost stepped on me earlier! How was I to know I was sleeping on his wall? I opened my eyes and before I had the chance to jump down, he spit at me and hit me square in the chest! Being spit on by a llama isn't a pleasant thing, and I do think it was rather uncalled for. I squawked and ran off around the corner to look for a place to preen and get myself cleaned up. Since it was dark, I knew it was probably time for church and I didn't want to go to church looking scraggly.

By the time I rushed back to the Plaza and arrived at the church, the service had already started. The doors were closed so I didn't have a chance to go inside and see how many other roosters were there, I had to be content with hiding in the bushes under a window where I heard the most beautiful music I had ever heard. There must have been misters and missuses in that church along with the roosters because no rooster I know can sing like that. It was peaceful and beautiful and when it was over I knew I had been a part of something special. When all those people poured out of church I stayed where I was expecting things to quiet down as people went home, but I was wrong about that. Not long after the church let out, the sky over the plaza lit up with a fireworks display that I will never forget. I'd seen fireworks before from our house on the hill, but this was close up and looked like spiky, exploding flowers in the sky. After it was over I was so tired that I scooted back under the window by the side of the church and fell asleep almost before I had my head tucked under my wing.

I woke up Christmas morning excited to see what the day would bring, but it was surprisingly quiet in the town. I roamed around and heard lots of happy voices coming from inside houses. Christmas day seemed to be a quiet day spent with your family at home. When I realized that, I got really homesick. I wondered what the other chickens were doing on our farm on the hillside. I wondered if my missus was making tamales and if Panchito was getting one of his daily baths. I knew I must be homesick if I was thinking about Panchito. I spent the rest of the day scratching around the church. I felt a little better when I found a few other chickens scratching around on the other side of the square- at least I wasn't totally alone on Christmas.

The day after Christmas I woke up under the church window to the wonderful sounds of people and vendors and the snorts of alpacas who had arrived at the plaza with their missuses. I spent most of the morning wandering around the plaza, searching everywhere for my missus and Panchito. I saw that rude, spitting llama and decided to stay as far away from him as I could. Just when I started to get worried that I would never get home again I heard a familiar scream. It was Panchito, fussing because another alpaca was eating his hay. I have never been so glad to hear Panchito's voice in my life. I snuck up behind him and while my missus's back was turned and Panchito was nipping at the other alpaca, I jumped up into the bolsa and settled in for the ride home.

Before I went to sleep that night, I walked to the edge of our yard and looked down the hill at the town of Cusco. I could see all the brightly colored lights and hear the church bells. I was happy to have had an adventure, but in the words of a wise missus from a faraway land, "there's no place like home."

Love, Cake, and Fried Chicken, Kochi, Japan, Present Day

C hristmas in Japan means three very important things. The first one is love. Everyone wants to be in love on Christmas Eve. My mister and missus have two teenage daughters and that's all they can talk about. Personally, I think love is silly. Sometimes my mister and missus walk in the field holding hands. That seems dangerous, my mister might stumble on a dirt clod and fall down on his face. How could he break his fall if his hands aren't free? Love just isn't practical.

Love is especially important at Christmas. On Christmas Eve everyone wants to be out on a date. I could go on a date if I wanted, I just don't want to. One time, I was scratching out behind the barn all by myself and our rooster came out there and started scratching around with me. He started making those little clucking sounds pretending he found something good for me to eat- please! I'm not going to fall for that! I think he thought we were on a date. But honestly, if I were to go on a date, I sure wouldn't go on a date behind the barn! If that rooster were to ever want to take me on a date, and I sure hope he never does, because, like I said, I don't want to go on any dates, the very least he could do would be to take me somewhere nice. It's not nice behind the barn, it smells bad back there. I'd insist we go somewhere special, like in the front yard where we have a cherry tree that blooms in springtime and smells lovely. That would be a good place for a date, if I ever did want to go on one...

The second thing that's very important in Japan at Christmas time is cake. My mister and missus grow strawberries because they need them to make our very tasty Japanese Christmas cake. Christmas wouldn't be Christmas without the traditional sponge cake with whipped cream and strawberries. My family makes so many cakes they can't eat them all, that's why they have to take them into the city so other people can eat them too. They take them to a Christmas market so they can share them with all of Kochi. Of course, no one could have a Christmas cake if it weren't for the eggs that my colleagues and I lay for them. Christmas cake is so important that I don't think Christmas could exist without it. That means that chickens are the most important part of Christmas because without our eggs there would be no cake. I suppose strawberries are important too, but not as much.

Someday I would like to go to the market in Kochi and see the looks of happiness on the faces of the people when they take a bite of my mister's Christmas cake made with my eggs. Laying eggs isn't exactly a pleasant experience, I think I would have the encouragement to keep doing it if I could see how much joy my eggs are bringing to my fellow citizens. I think laying eggs for Christmas cake is my special way of contributing to the Christmas festivities.

The third important thing you need for Christmas in Japan is dinner, and in Japan that means one thing- fried chicken. All of Japan eats fried chicken for dinner on Christmas Eve or Christmas day, every year. From what I've heard, the best fired chicken comes from a place called Kentucky. I have never actually met a chicken from Kentucky, so I don't know much about them. I think Kentucky might be near Tokyo since it must be a very big place to have enough chickens to feed all of Japan. Sometimes I wonder how chickens from Kentucky feel about being Christmas dinner. I know they must be proud because, though I hate to admit it, it's possible that they might even be more important than cake since everyone knows that you can't eat cake until after you've eaten dinner. It's kind of like a "which came first, the chicken or the egg" kind of situation. I wonder if being Christmas dinner is such a grand thing that the fried chickens from Kentucky don't mind getting eaten? I've always been glad that I was hatched in Kochi instead of Kentucky, but maybe I'm wrong to feel that way. We all have a purpose, I just hope that laying eggs for Christmas cake is important enough. I'm an ambitious bird so I need to make sure I'm achieving great things.

The last few days before Christmas were a whirlwind of activity on our farm. Everyone was either picking strawberries, or making cakes, or driving the truck full of cakes to town. I did my best to lay an egg a day, no one could ever accuse me of being a slacker. It was in the middle of all that activity that the accident happened. It happened when my missus rushed out of the house and hopped up on the tractor and took off into the field. I don't see my missus driving the tractor very much, so maybe that's why she lost control of it and flipped it over in a ditch while she was still sitting on the seat. We heard a rumble and a crash and then my missus started screaming. Chickens like routine, we like everything to be predictable. So, when the accident happened it made us scared and nervous, that's why we started to fuss. A chicken fussing sounds like a long, higher pitched cluck, and a lot of chickens fussing sounds like a racket. Our noisy outbursts made my mister come out of the house to holler at us, but over our noise he heard his missus scream. That's when I saw it. His face changed. His face was a mix of fear and shock and something else, could it have been love? My mister took off running full speed across the field toward the sound of my missus. In barely a minute or two we saw him pick our missus up out of the dirt and sprint back with her in his arms, shouting for his helpers as he ran. They placed her in the back seat of the car and off they went, the tires spitting gravel as they sped down the dirt road.

I was a little worried when it first happened, but then a friend of mine found some rotten strawberries that were filled with ants, so I forgot about my missus for a while. I was reminded when late that afternoon they came home, my missus had her leg wrapped up in a thick, white bandage. She put her arms around my mister's neck as he carried her into the house. My mister must have had a sore back from all that carrying my missus around, she's a full-sized missus, not a bantam.

Somehow all the helpers and my mister got the cakes to town in time for Christmas Eve. After the last truck left, I watched the two teenage daughters giggle and pose for pictures in their fancy dresses as their young misters took them away in a car, probably going out to dinner to eat a fried chicken from Kentucky and a Christmas cake made with my exceptional eggs.

As early evening came on and we started to head back to the coop for the night I paused in front of the house so I could look in the window and check on my missus. I saw her and my mister sitting at the table with a pretty red tablecloth and a candle lit in the middle of the table. They were dressed nicely, and my missus had her injured leg propped up on a chair next to her. They were having dinner and smiling at each other, and every now and then they would reach across the table and hold hands. It looked so peaceful and nice it made me think that being in love on Christmas Eve wasn't such a bad thing after all. Just then our rooster walked past me and clucked at me to pick up the pace. He's bossy, but maybe, just maybe, when springtime rolls around, I'll scratch around under the cherry blossom tree with him. That might be nice.

Slap Some Prawns on the Barbie, Canberra, Australia, Present Day

I don't like kangaroos. I don't like them because they're always trying to get attention. For example, they could walk like everyone else, but instead they hop just because they want to be special and get attention. And if that weren't enough, they carry their babies around in a pouch just so everyone can see it and think that's cute. My babies come out of an egg, that's almost the same as a pouch, isn't it? But since chickens are good mothers, we don't let our babies stay in the egg, we get them up and scratching around on day one. Roo babies are helpless, they ride around in that pouch for who knows how long. They just want to be pampered and taken care of. Talk about entitled. Yes, roos are definitely irritating. We should slap one of them on the barbie for Christmas lunch, that's what I say.

Today is Christmas Eve. I heard my missus say that there are some places in the world where it's cold at Christmas time, that sounds awful! I feel bad for people who can't have a backyard barbeque on Christmas. And how do these people go swimming and surfing if it's cold outside? I don't surf myself, but that's only because they don't make surfboards small enough for me. The fact that it's warm and beautiful at Christmas time just proves what I've always known is true, Australia is awesome.

For me, the most important part about Christmas is the food. My mister and his sons own a fish market and everyone goes crazy for seafood at Christmas around here, especially prawns. Some folks can't even have Christmas without prawns, I don't blame them, prawns are tasty- not that I ever get to taste one, we usually sell out before noon on Christmas Eve. Then, since they're out of prawns, the family has something boring, like ham, for Christmas lunch. Who wants ham? Ham doesn't have eyes and a face like prawns and grasshoppers and baby frogs! The tastiest things have eyes and faces, everyone knows that!

After Christmas lunch the family will gather in the yard for a dumb game of cricket. The whole country is crazy for cricket. I'm as good an Aussie as anyone and I've watched about a million cricket matches in my time and did you know I have never once seen an actual cricket? What kind of game calls itself cricket but then doesn't have any crickets? If I have to eat leftover ham for Christmas lunch it would go down easier if I had a nice cricket or two to add as a garnish.

I know I sound grumpy, but that's only because Christmas can be a hard time of the year if you don't have any family. I know I have my mates, they're good mates. We scratch around together and sleep up on the roost together at night, but it's just not the same as having a family. I must have a mother somewhere, but for the life of me, I can't remember much about her. I also have a vague memory of being a mother myself, but how could I forget about my own chicks? Sometimes I look around on the roost at night and wonder if any of those full-grown hens were once my chicks. What kind of mother actually forgets her own chicks? Christmas is a time for family, and I don't have any.

Since I was a tad bit melancholy I decided to spend the afternoon alone, scratching out by the fence. I could hear the voices and laughter coming from the house, everyone was probably enjoying family time, eating their ham and wearing the funny paper crowns they always wear at Christmas. It would be hours before my missus would get around to bringing us our feast of table scraps. So, I thought it would be best if I spent the time scratching for Christmas beetles under a Christmas bush. Yes, Australians love Christmas so much we actually have a beetle, and a bush, named after it.

I was so deep in thought that instead of being cautious when I came to a high point on the fence, I just scrunched down and went underneath it without thinking. That's why I was surprised when I heard a noise and looked up and saw a kangaroo standing a few metres away- staring at me. I was so shocked that I stood frozen, just staring back and wondering if roos were fond of chicken dinners. While I was staring, suddenly, a joey popped up in the pouch and gave me a look. What was that expression on its face? Hunger? I didn't know what to do, but just then, I heard the noise that would save my life.

On the other side of the fence stood our rooster. He must have noticed that I was missing and came looking for me! He started cackling and fussing and pacing on the fence line. Before I knew it, the rest of the flock rushed over, and everyone started fussing at the top of their lungs. That brought my missus and the rest of the family out of the house to save me. Or maybe it was time for the cricket game, either way, I was glad to see them. My mister lifted one of the little boys over the fence to chase me back under, that made me emotional, they were willing to risk that child's life just to save me! Everyone knows kangaroos eat children! I was glad he was there to chase me because I had forgotten how I got on that side of the fence to begin with. Once I scooted back under, everyone clapped and headed to the yard where they picked up their cricket bats and got ready to play. While they were choosing up teams my missus went into the house and came back out with the lunch scraps. She called to us in a high-pitched voice and we ran over. To my amazement there was no ham, I saw nothing but faces. There must have been hundreds of prawn heads! The family had prawns for lunch and saved the heads just for us!

As I munched on prawn heads I glanced around at my mates, both feathered and human and I thought that maybe it was fine to not have a family for Christmas. It's another Aussie tradition to have a celebration at Christmas called Friendmas. I never understood until just now how important it is to have friends at Christmas time. Maybe my mates were every bit as good as a real family, and maybe they were even better. Merry Chrissie everyone!

Out to Sea, Corfu, Greece, Present Day

C all me Ishmael. My mister says he gave me that name because he knows I was born to be on the sea. He's right about that. I was hatched on land, but things weren't working out for me too well, so I became a sailor. I'm a small rooster and the other roosters in our flock were picking on me. One morning they cornered me by the side of the house and were spurring me something awful. My mister was heading out to his boat and saw what was happening, so he scooped me up and took me out on his charter. I think he thought I would just stay in the cabin and not bother his guests, but I got curious and wandered out to where he was helping his guests fish for tuna. Those people thought it was funny to see a chicken on a boat and they all wanted their picture taken with me. Ever since that day I go with him whenever he has a charter and help him entertain the guests. He says I'm good for business. I love the sweet smell of the sea and when we hit a small wave the boat bounces and I can feel the sea breeze ruffling my feathers. I also love the seafood bits and pieces that the guests toss to me while they're dining on the fabulous lunch Alexander, our deckhand, cooks for us. Yes, life on the sea is the only life for me.

Since it's Christmas time here in Corfu I haven't been out on the water much. My mister likes to celebrate the holidays with his family and there aren't as many tourists in town that need to go fishing. I don't mind staying on land this time of year because my missus makes the best melomakarona cookies and she always makes sure she bakes extra for the chickens. I would miss out on that if I were out sailing. Plus, since we were home on Christmas Eve morning, I got to hear the kalanda carols being sung by the neighborhood children. They got to our house early since they knew my missus was good at baking and they would get the best treats as a reward for their songs here. As my missus passed around the plate of melomakaronas to the children I thought maybe she should have come out to our coop and gathered some eggs for the carolers as well. Everyone loves eggs and those children were probably just too shy to ask for one. Maybe if word got around that my missus was handing out eggs, we'd have every kalanda singer in Corfu at our house next year!

On Christmas day I spent most of my time on the porch since I was trying to avoid those mean roosters who are jealous of me and my seafaring ways. That's when I had the opportunity to hop up on the windowsill and look into the window at the family celebrating with their loved ones. I've heard that nowadays many trendy families drag a tree into the house and decorate it with lights for the holiday, but at my house we still decorate a wooden boat. I got to see ours sitting on the table all lit up and sparkly. It looked beautiful and I know that on New Year's Day there will be gifts by the boat for the children from a wonderful man named Saint Basil. He always brings gifts, but not until New Years Day, Christmas Day is for church and family.

While I was on the porch, I also got a good look at the pomegranate my mister hung over the doorway. Pomegranates are one of my favorite treats and I hope we don't have to go fishing on New Year's Day because I want to be here when they smash that pomegranate on the ground. The more seeds it has, the more luck the family will have. Also, the more seeds, the more yum for the chickens. It's our job to clean up the pomegranate after it's been smashed. We don't mind.

So far the Christmas season has been great, but today we have a charter so we're off to the harbor to take some tourists out tuna fishing. My mister says this isn't the best time of year to fish for tuna, but the guests don't need to know that. I think Alexander will bring along some shrimp for lunch in case the guests don't catch anything we can cook. I'm excited to get back out on the water where I belong, I'm just worried about one thing- the kallikantzaroi.

I wasn't worried about the kallikantzaroi when I was at home because my missus always puts a colander on the porch to confuse them. They aren't good counters and all those holes in the colander confuse them. I've heard they can't even count to three. How dumb! Even a chicken can count! I have three eyes and eleven toes on each foot. But I guess not every creature is as smart as a chicken... The kallikantzaroi are shaggy little goblins who live under the ground and come to the surface between Christmas and New Years to play pranks on people. I'm a bit suspicious of this, I've done a lot of scratching in my life and I've never seen one under the dirt with the worms. I wonder how the worms feel about sharing the dirt with those little mischievous creatures? I'm worried about what could happen if they dig themselves up out of the dirt and then decide to hop on our boat.

Our charter started out well, my mister introduced me as his first mate and I saw Alexander make a face at that, I'm sure he thought HE was the first mate instead of just the cook. Honestly, folks shouldn't think more highly of themselves than they ought to. While we were heading out, I busied myself on the boat searching for kallikantzaroi. I looked everywhere I thought they could be hiding, but I didn't see any, maybe that's why I was off guard when the pranks started.

The first thing that happened was one of our guests started to act silly and almost fell overboard. He'd been drinking a lot of water from a glass bottle instead of a plastic bottle like everyone else, maybe those kallikantzaroi switched his water for ouzo! I've seen what ouzo can do to a person. No one would ever drink ouzo on purpose. My mister had to send him inside the cabin to lie down for a while since he might scare away what few tunas there might be out there if he went floundering around in the water this time of the year. Then, one of the ladies got excited when she thought she had hooked something and started jumping up and down and her sunglasses fell right off her head and into the water. She got upset and wanted her mister to jump in after them because she said they were expensive, but even I know she was exaggerating. My mister and I have walked past the souvenir shop on the corner enough times to see the sunglasses selling for a couple of Euros and that's not valuable enough to go diving for sunglasses. I wasn't sure how the kallikantzaroi were involved with that mishap, but I was worried just the same. The last thing that happened showed me for sure that the kallikantzaroi were definitely on the boat with us. Alexander burned the shrimp. He said he got distracted and wasn't paying attention, even though last time I checked he had ONE job to do and that was to cook the shrimp. He had to serve fresh salads and wine instead of shrimp salads. I'm sure those kallikantzaroi made Alexander think there was something important to look at on his cell phone when he should have been looking at the shrimp.

We finally made it back to the wharf in one piece. No one caught anything and everyone was a bit hungry, but they seemed happy as they wished us kalá Christoúgenna and hauled the sleepy, ouzo drinking man off the boat with them.

My mister chuckled all the way home as he carried me up the darkening street. I liked that time of the evening in Corfu, I could see the brightly lit boats through the windows of the homes we passed. I could even see some Christmas trees in the windows of the folks who wanted to be modern and stylish. I could smell the delicious aroma of the Vasilopita cake coming from every home and I knew tomorrow must be New Years Day. Tomorrow, everyone will get a piece of cake and in one piece there will be a coin. Whoever gets that piece will have good luck for the whole year. Maybe the coin will be in the bits and pieces that get thrown to the chickens. If I get the coin, I'll buy some sunglasses to keep on board our charter, so we have a replacement in case those kallikantzaroi get up to their old tricks again next year. But for now, I know I need my rest. Tomorrow is New Year's Day which means presents for the children and pomegranate for the chickens. What could be better than that?

A Chicken Carol, London, England 1843

I hate Christmas. Christmas is nothing more than a commercial holiday dreamed up by all the shopkeepers so they can get everyone's money. I don't have any money, but if I did you wouldn't catch me spending it on a bunch of presents for other people. If a person works hard and earns something they should get to have it for themselves.

I almost started to like Christmas a little bit on account of all the extra treats that come our way. My missus is fond of baking at Christmas time, and she always saves some extra cookies or a piece of cake to give just to the chickens. When she tosses me a piece of something good, she calls me her, "little, grumpy, girl." Humph, she thinks she's endearing herself to me by giving me a cute name, but it just reinforces what I already know, she's as dumb as a wooden spoon.

The proof is that if she spends all her time baking for other people. She should keep the results for herself, not throw it to the chickens.

I'm in an unusually bad mood today on account of a dream I had last night. I think all this jolly Christmas tomfoolery has affected me worse than I thought. I dreamt about an old hen who used to live with us a year or so ago. She was mean, even meaner than I am. One time, my missus burned the tops of a whole tray of biscuits. Instead of cutting the tops off and serving them to the family, she tossed them to us. See what I mean by dumb? Well, I was a young pullet then and had never tasted biscuits before, I ran over with everyone else but that mean old hen charged in and attacked anyone who even got near the biscuits. A couple of the quicker hens were able to grab one and take off with it, but most of us didn't even get a bite. She stood there and ate every one of them herself, chasing off anyone who dared to come near. That's how it was with her, everyone hated her.

When we woke up one morning and found her dead on the floor, we didn't keep our distance like we would usually do if it had been someone else. We all just started scratching around and scratched our litter all over her body. When the yard boy opened the coop and let us out for the day he simply walked in and picked her body up by the legs and hurled her over the fence into the gutter. He didn't even bury her. Later that day I saw neighborhood dogs tearing around with her. I don't know why I dreamed about her, like I said, all this Christmas humbug is getting to me...

Later that afternoon I was thoroughly disgusted when my missus came out for her daily visit and promptly scooped up Lucinda and sat down on a bench with her. Lucinda is a pathetic little hen with a crippled leg. I don't know if her leg got bent in the shell when she was hatched or if her mother stepped on her and injured her, but Lucinda wobbles around and would have had a rough go of it if my missus hadn't decided to make her a pet. It's pathetic the way my missus fawns over her and brings her special treats. Personally, I think Lucinda should have been culled when she was a chick, it probably would have been a mercy to her, and it certainly would have been nicer for all of us to not have to look at her all the time. Besides, with one less mouth to feed there would be more food for us.

That scene of the missus and Lucinda put me in a foul mood, so I wandered over under a bush for a nap, that's when I had another dream. I dreamed about my life when I was a small chick. I remembered my mama and what a good mama she was. I remembered how wonderful it felt to be safe and warm with my brothers and sisters under her feathers. I recalled the time she chased off a feral cat that was trying to catch us and eat us. She taught us how to scratch around and scoop up beetles and roaches. In my dream I saw how my mama would grab one, but instead of eating it herself, she would give it to us. I thought she was the best mama on all the earth, that's why when I was grown and the urge to sit on eggs came over me, I was excited to be a mama myself. I wanted to be just like her. But as I sat on those eggs, I couldn't help thinking about all the beetles I was missing out on. After a week of sitting, I abandoned my eggs and never went back. There was simply too much that I was missing by trying to be a mama.

Chickens don't sweat but when I woke up from that dream I was in a panic. The sun was low in the sky, it was almost dark and I should've been in the coop by then. I got up but felt unsteady on my feet. The dream had shaken me. I don't know why I remembered all that, surely it was the right decision to leave my eggs and live for myself!

As I settled up on the roost, I noticed that once I sat down, the other hens moved away from me. That's how I liked it, but why was it bothering me now? I glanced out the window and saw my mister heading out into the twilight. My mister was a writer and he liked to write his stories in his head while he walked the streets of London at night. Writing is stupid. Maybe my mister should give it up and get a real job so we could all have biscuits every day. That was my last thought before I fell asleep.

In my dream I saw Lucinda. She was hobbling around our yard, and she fell. Then I saw myself. I trampled all over Lucinda, and because I led the way, the other chickens trampled on her too. She tried to get up, but she couldn't. Then the snow began to fall and all of us ran to the warm shelter of the coop, leaving Lucinda behind. Later that afternoon I saw my missus come out and kneel in the snow next to Lucinda's body. I saw her weep. I ran out of the coop to stand before my missus. I wanted to comfort her somehow and let her know that she could pet me now and I would be her new favorite, but my missus just looked at me with cold eyes and said, "Isn't this what you wanted? One less mouth to feed and more food for yourself?"

I woke up when the rooster crowed with a feeling of dread. I looked quickly around at my coop-mates in the half light of dawn and saw Lucinda sitting on the straw on the ground with her head tucked under her wing. She always sat there on the ground alone, as close as she could get to all of us. She couldn't climb up onto the roost with that bad foot of hers. Such a sad existence.

That afternoon I decided to shake off all these terrible dreams I had been having and get out of my melancholy mood. I was determined to take a soothing dust bath to calm my nerves and give me the strength to get through the day. I knew it was Christmas Eve and I just didn't have the stomach for all the Christmas balderdash. The problem was that it was so cold that the ground was too hard to scratch up some dirt for my bath, but I knew of a place where the ground was softer. I walked to the back of our yard where our property meets the property of the neighbors who live behind us. The neighbor mister had pulled up a dead bramble bush a fortnight ago. It was the perfect spot.

After a few minutes I was covered in cool dirt, and I could feel all the tense holiday foolishness fading away. I felt peaceful for the first time in weeks- until the neighbor children started throwing rocks. I should have thought of that ahead of time, I knew those children hated me. One time I chased one of them and when he tripped over a tree root I was able to draw blood with a couple of hard pecks to his forearm, now he would have his revenge. I leaped up when the rocks started pelting me, I could hear their cruel jeers as I ran for the safety of my own yard, but then a sharp rock hit me square on the side of my head and I felt myself tumble head over feet and everything went black.

In my dream I saw our chicken yard on Christmas morning. We could hear the delighted sounds of the children coming from the house. They were unwrapping their gifts and enjoying the treats Father Christmas left for them in their stockings. Then my missus came out to the yard with an entire mincemeat pie just for all the chickens! As she set it down on the ground and cheerfully called out a Merry Christmas, everyone came running. That's when I saw myself. I wasn't running. I was lying on the ground with blood coming from a wound on my head. Surely everyone would walk around me, but they didn't. They trampled all over me. I waited for my missus to pick me up and feed me even the smallest piece of pie crust. But instead, she used the toe of her boot to nudge me out of the way. After everyone, even Lucinda, had had their fill of pie they gathered around my missus as she pet each one of them and sang Christmas carols to them. I lay there behind them, cold and forgotten.

I awakened as gentle hands lifted me and held me close. My missus used the hem of her apron to wipe the blood from the side of my head where the rock that stunned me had opened up a small wound. I could hear my mister talking sternly to the neighbor boys about how there was enough cruelty in this world, and what was needed was more kindness and concern for others.

As my senses began to return to me, I watched as my missus carried me back to our yard. I was surprised to see all of my coop-mates, even Lucinda gathered around in a group, anxious to see if I was alright. I heard my missus marvel as she explained to my mister that she never would have known I was in trouble if the rest of the flock hadn't put up a fuss. She set me down and though I was a bit unsteady, I could walk slowly, and I noticed that no one shied away from me, they all seemed glad to see that I was better. My missus checked on me periodically the rest of the day, and I felt safe and warm, like I did when I was a chick.

That evening instead of hopping up on the roost with everyone else, I settled down next to Lucinda on the floor. Some may have thought it was because I was still dizzy from my ordeal, but really, it was because I didn't want Lucinda to feel alone on Christmas. I even let her tuck her head into my shoulder feathers so she would be extra warm.

I decided that from that time on I would be a changed hen. I decided that I would honor Christmas in my heart and try to keep it all the year. I would never forget the lessons the dreams taught me, and I would be a better hen to all. As I closed my eyes, I could hear the sweet songs of a group of wassailers as they wandered down our street mixed with the sounds of laughter and joy. As the hens around me clucked softly and settled in for the night I felt a feeling of contentment like I had never felt before. With Lucinda's warm breath ruffling my feathers and the bright stars twinkling through the coop window I sighed and thought to myself, "God bless us every one."

Advent Calendars and Potato Dumplings, Munich, Germany 1919

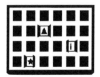

I'm a paste eater. I know I shouldn't eat paste because if I eat too much of it, it will glue my insides together, but I can't help it. The children like to do their crafts out on a table in the front yard so when they run inside to get a snack I hop up on the table and help myself. My missus makes the paste herself from wheat flour and water. I think it's tasty.

Today I got yelled at because I ate most of the paste the children were using to glue the pieces on their advent calendar. They each have their own calendar because that's what my mister does for his living- he makes advent calendars and sells them to people to make their Christmas extra merry. An advent calendar is a piece of cardboard with twenty-four boxes. There is also a piece of paper with twenty-four pictures. You cut out a picture every day and glue it on the box for that day. Most of the pictures are of something called the nativity scene. So far, my favorite picture is one of a group of animals looking at baby Jesus in his manger. I like to look at all the pictures while I'm eating paste, they're very beautiful and heartwarming. One time I had an accident on the advent calendar while I was up on the table enjoying my lunch of paste. When the littlest girl saw what I had done she started to cry. I'm more careful now.

One day I heard my mister telling his children the story of where he got the idea for making an advent calendar. Apparently, his mother would use chalk to make twenty-four marks on the door frame and he got to wipe off one mark every day until it was Christmas day. Then his mother realized that the marks on the door frame idea was a little boring, so she made twenty-four cookies and attached those to a board and then my mister got to eat a cookie every day leading up to Christmas! That's an idea I can get behind. Maybe my mister could make an advent calendar for the chicken coop with twenty-four grasshoppers attached to it. I bet that would be a big seller because of how much people love their chickens.

Though everyone liked the two-piece advent calendar, my mister really found success in his business when he got the idea to put the pictures behind little doors on the calendar. That way, there was no cutting and pasting necessary. Though the public liked this idea a lot, I hated it because I looked forward to eating paste every year at Christmas time. It's a tradition that I wanted to pass on to my own chicks when I have some someday. Now they will never know the joy of jumping up on the table and helping themselves to a snack while they gaze at the beautiful pictures the children are cutting out. The worst part about all this is that my mister actually got the idea for the doors from me!

I consider myself the most intelligent chicken in our whole coop. I'm not bragging, it's not prideful if it's a fact. I'm the smartest because I'm the chicken who figured out how to get extra food from the missus. My missus is the person in the family who makes the meals, so I thought that if I could cozy up to her, she might give me some extra bits and pieces here and there. My plan worked. It's a little sad that my missus thinks I run to her and jump up on her lap when she's sitting on the porch because I like her, I just do it because of the treats. My missus makes the best Kässpatzn in all of Munich. Kässpatzn are noodles that taste like cheese. Noodles used to be worms before they were noodles so of course, chickens love any kind of noodles they can get. I also can never turn down my missus's Christmas stollen. She puts raisins and walnuts in it and there's absolutely nothing better. Sometimes she brings a piece of stollen with her out on the porch and if you have to guess who eats more of it, me or her, well then you don't know chickens at all.

One day I got tired of waiting for my missus to come outside so I could pretend to love her when all I really love is her food. It was a couple of days before Christmas and from the smell of it I could tell she was making one of my favorite dishes- knoedel. What's not to love about potato dumplings? I was patient as long as chickenly possible before I just couldn't stand it anymore. I hopped up on the porch, marched over to the door, and started pecking on the door to try and get her attention. Afterall, what did she expect me to do? If she was going to torture me with the smell of her famous Christmas knoedel, then she deserved to get the paint on her door chipped off by my beak.

It didn't take long before she came to investigate who was knocking at her door. When she looked down and saw me, her whole face lit up with a smile and she clapped her hands and used the silly voice she uses when she talks to her baby. She stooped down and said all sorts of endearing things to me. Then she rushed back into the kitchen and came back with exactly what I was hoping for, a nice plate of knoedel with a slice of Bavarian pumpernickel bread on the side. It tasted way better than paste.

Since that worked so well, I began to peck at her front door daily, and I was rewarded with something tasty to eat each time. I started to gain some weight because usually chickens burn a lot of calories scratching around for bugs, but I had no reason to scratch when I was getting fed like a king every day on the porch. Out of gratitude, and to keep the gravy train rolling, I sat in her lap when the opportunity presented itself and gagged a little when I heard her introduce me to a neighbor as her "best friend." So sad.

It was between the Christmas and New Year holidays that I overheard my mister excitedly telling my missus his new idea for an advent calendar for next year. My mister was always creating new and improved calendars, Christmas had only been over for a couple of days and here he was already planning for next year. My missus interrupted him and told him that instead of all the fuss with paste and scissors, he should create little doors so that when you open them, you see the beautiful picture inside. She laughed and told him the story about how I peck at the door every day and get rewarded for my efforts. Well, he really liked that idea, in fact, he liked it so much that he ran off down the street in the direction of his office to get working on it right away.

I had to stop and contemplate the situation for a moment, if there's no more need for cutting and pasting advent calendars then my future offspring will not be paste-eaters like I am. That's a shame because I'm sure that all that paste has made me the unusually smart hen I am today. But I guess instead of teaching them to eat paste I will just need to teach them to pretend to love the missus and peck at her door like I do. Maybe the mister will get the idea to attach a piece of knoedel behind the doors on the calendar so that the children of Munich can have a potato dumpling every single day leading up to Christmas! I'll miss the paste, but everyone knows that knoedel is a lot tastier than paste anyways.

The Hygge Egg Song, Ringkøbing, Denmark, Present Day

H ere in Denmark, Christmas is all about hygge. Hygge isn't a thing, it's a way of life. It means fun and happiness with good people. Some examples of hygge are when the hen sitting on the roost next to me doesn't mind when I shove my head into her tail feathers to keep warm. Hygge is when the missus throws us the cut tops of tomatoes and there's enough for everyone to have at least one. And hygge is when the rooster accidentally gets locked in the coop and we can enjoy a day without him bothering us. I'm told that Christmas is a whole month of the best hygge there is, I can't wait!

Since this is my first Christmas, I've been enjoying learning all the Danish Christmas traditions. The first tradition I learned was all about the nisser living up in the attic. I heard the children talking about them and apparently, they're up there in the month of

December to spy on the children and make sure that they're behaving themselves. Though I think it's kind of creepy that small elf-like creatures are stalking the children, I've noticed a positive change in the children's attitudes. The children are usually always chasing me around trying to catch me and hold me like I'm the cat or something. Honestly, like I've got time for that? Insects don't just march up to me and say, "Eat me please." I have to hunt them down and scratch them up out of the dirt. If the children are carrying me around all day, then everyone else will get all the good bugs and I'll be left with nothing but ants. Ants are so small that it isn't even worth the effort to peck for them, plus, they don't taste all that good. I'm grateful to the nisser for making the children behave. Now I don't have to be worried about being hauled all over the yard wrapped in a doll blanket. It's humiliating.

I wonder what the nisser do all day up in the attic? They probably eat attic spiders. Eating spiders is one of my favorite things. The nisser probably eat the spiders they find in the attic because they're hungry. The family doesn't feed them until Christmas Eve when they leave a bowl of Risengrød out for them to eat. I guess in the weeks before Christmas they must either eat spiders or starve. I wouldn't mind that- spiders are crunchy.

Christmas isn't just about the nisser, I've also noticed that Christmas seems to be all about candles. The family has gone absolutely crazy for candles. Their whole house is full of candles, they've even dragged a tree inside from the woods and attached some candles to it. The tree also has lots of paper hearts and Danish flags hanging on it along with the candles. It's only a matter of time before the tree, and the whole house, goes up in smoke.

Another thing that seems very important to everyone is counting down the days until Christmas, this involves, you guessed it, more candles. They call the countdown candles "advent candles." They light one every Sunday. I'm not good at counting, but I think that once they light that last candle it will be Christmas Eve. I used to wonder what would happen if they forgot to light the candle one day, would they miss Christmas? But, as it turns out, the candles aren't the only countdown method they use. Everyone in the family also has their very own julekalender. The julekalender has a treat behind every door and you get to open one door a day. The children have a piece of chocolate every day before Christmas. The mother and father must get thirsty with all the Christmas preparations because their julekalenders have tiny bottles for each day. If they're thirsty they should just drink a whole glass of water, those tiny bottles don't look like they hold much. And oh, if you accidentally burn down all your candles, eat all your chocolate, and drink all your bottles, you will still know how many days until Christmas because the television has a show with a different episode for every day counting up to Christmas Eve. Chickens don't watch television, we're much too busy for that.

On Christmas Eve everyone waits for a Christmas man they call Julemand. Julemand heads up to the attic and chats with the nisser, the nisser tell him if the children have been good or not and if they've been good, they get presents. I wonder if that applies to chickens too. I've noticed that chickens seem to be ignored at Christmas time around here. I couldn't help but be offended when I found out that whoever finds the almond in their rice pudding gets a marzipan pig for their prize. Why a pig? Why not a marzipan chicken? Marzipan can be made to look like chickens, why hasn't that happened? And what about Christmas dinner? I've heard that everyone eats roast duck for Christmas dinner! Why duck and not chicken? Everyone knows that chickens are much tastier than ducks. Oh wait... never mind.

Though I've really enjoyed all the little traditions that have happened so far, I still wasn't feeling the Christmas hygge like I thought I would. In fact, it wasn't until Christmas Eve after dinner, that the hygge happened. That's when the family decided to celebrate the holiday in the true chicken way- by singing.

Chickens are big singers. We don't sing well and no one would categorize us as "song birds," but we're enthusiastic and we sing when we have a good reason to. We sing when we've laid an egg. Laying an egg is a great accomplishment. I can't be sure, but I don't think anyone in the family has ever laid an egg. I also haven't heard of the nisser or Mister Julemand laying eggs. Laying eggs is our thing and we make sure the whole world knows about it when it happens. The song is like a loud cluck with a drawn out bawk afterwards, then we start again. The best part is that oftentimes, when one hen starts to sing, we all decide to sing along with her. Sometimes we stand around the nesting box where she has just accomplished her great endeavor, and we all sing together to celebrate. It's something I thought was unique to chickens, but that was because I had never seen what goes on after Christmas dinner in the house with the family.

Usually, I'm in the coop by the time it gets dark, but out of curiosity I wandered over to the willow tree and hopped up on a branch so I could see into the window. I was hoping to see the nisser chasing some spiders around, but what I saw was much better, it was magical.

The whole family, including the grandparents and aunts, uncles, and cousins, were holding hands and dancing around the Christmas tree! It was a bit awkward looking, but they seemed happy. Maybe I shouldn't judge their dancing skills since chickens aren't big dancers. Our rooster likes to dance a bit to try and impress us, but we just ignore him. But it wasn't their dancing that got my attention, it was the singing. They were singing an egg song. I say that because remember when I said chickens don't sound like songbirds? Well, the family didn't sound great either, especially Uncle Valdemar. He was singing at the top of his voice, but I don't think he really knew the words or the tune because he would sing through the pauses and sing words that were different from what everyone else sang. This made everyone laugh and I knew I was witnessing something very special- what I saw was the Christmas hygge I'd heard so much about.

As Christmas time winds up and we all get ready to make it through the rest of our long winter, I think that the hygge way of life will be something I try to live daily. When it's snowing outside and we can't go out and scratch for bugs, instead of being disappointed I will try and focus on how cozy it is in our coop when we're all together, safe and warm. And I know that when someone lays an egg, and we all start the egg song together, I'll feel warm in my heart. Afterall, there's nothing more hyggelig than gathering with those you love and singing a song about how great it is to lay an egg.

The Wise Chicken, Barcelona, Spain, Present Day

I t was never a goal of mine to become a king, but now that I am one, I can't imagine going back to the life of a commoner. I became a king by accident last Christmas, and I learned that in order to be a king there are two requirements. The first is you must be wise, and the second is you have to have a lot of candy.

Last year was my first Christmas and I enjoyed all the traditions that the family celebrated even though some of them were a bit unusual. First there was El Gordo. When someone told me about it, I thought folks were talking about me since I've put on some weight lately. It's not my fault. My missus has been doing a lot of baking for the holidays and she isn't the best baker, so the chickens end up getting a lot of burnt and odd tasting sweets. Eventually I found out El Gordo isn't me, it's something called a lottery and it's a way for someone to get a lot of extra money. Chickens don't use money so

I'm not sure what the fuss is about having a lot of it. The El Gordo lottery kicks the holiday season off and the strange thing about it is that everyone gives money but only one person gets money back. That doesn't sound like the best idea to me.

After El Gordo was over it was time for Christmas Eve. It would have been a wonderful and perfect day if it weren't for how mad I got over Tió de Nadal. Maybe I should have protested when I saw the family carry a smiley faced log into the house. That afternoon, my missus was giving us some burnt polvorones from the kitchen door, so I got to see straight into the dining room and was more than a little shocked to see that log sitting on the table covered with a blanket and wearing a cheery red hat. Chickens aren't allowed in the house but dead tree logs are? I heard the children talking about Tió and apparently, on Christmas morning they will beat him with a stick and sing a song to him, and in return he will poop out some presents for them- right there on the table! I once got in trouble for having an accident on the porch. I didn't even do it on purpose and I got yelled at, but the freaky faced log gets to relieve himself on the kitchen table and everyone thinks it's cute? Now that I'm a king I can safely say that we definitely won't be carrying on that tradition next year.

The next special day was el Día de Los Santos Inocentes. It happens a few days after Christmas day and it's a time when everyone plays tricks on each other. I played a trick on my missus, I laid an egg then turned around and used my beak to crack it open and then I ate it. Then I went around to the other nesting boxes and ate everyone else's eggs too. My stomach hurt after that, maybe I really am El Gordo...

Next came New Year's Eve and the twelve grapes. Chickens love grapes and after my missus counted out enough grapes for all her guests to have twelve each, she gave the rest to us. My missus must be confused about what makes a good grape- either that or she doesn't really like her guests all that much. I know that because she gave us the best grapes- the squishy ones. Who wants a hard grape? I was supposed to save my grapes for when the town clock struck midnight, then eat my grapes one at a time every time the clock struck so I could have good luck in the new year, but I fell asleep way before midnight. There was no use staying up when I had already eaten all my grapes (and some I snuck from the other chickens too).

After the New Year's celebrations, I thought the holiday season was basically over, I didn't know that the best was yet to come. On January 6th the kings arrive. We call it Día de los Reyes Magos and it's when the town has a big parade and the three kings ride on giant floats throwing candy to all the children. The three kings are also known as the Wise Men who came to visit the baby Jesus after he was born. I've put some thought into why they were known as wise, I think it's because they didn't show up on the day Jesus was born, they came a couple of weeks later. This is wise because although I don't know a lot about how human babies are born, I do get the feeling that the last thing a mama wants is to have strangers around when she's having a baby. Humans should have their babies in eggs like chickens do, it's a lot less messy. I think somehow those wise men knew that if they waited a couple of weeks to visit, it would give Mary time to rest up a bit.

To be a king you not only have to be wise, you have to give gifts. I'm a big believer in giving gifts, in fact, I give my eggs to my missus every single day (except for that one day when I ate them). Since I love my mister too, sometimes I like to give him an egg by leaving it in a place where only he can find it- like the seat of his tractor. One time I did that, and I guess he didn't see it on the seat and he sat right down on it. Let's just say that what he had to say about that wasn't exactly festive.

Luckily, the Christmas kings don't throw eggs at the crowds of children, they throw candy. Since I'm planning on being a king again next Christmas, I've started saving up candy to throw at the children for next year. I have two pieces already. I found one piece laying in the street a couple of weeks ago. It wasn't wrapped, but that's not a problem, grasshoppers and centipedes don't come wrapped and everyone knows how tasty they are. I was able to secure another piece of candy just yesterday when one of the children left it outside in the backyard on a rock next to the cars and trucks he was playing with. When he ran in the house I sprinted out and grabbed it. I saw him looking for it a little later and he started crying when he couldn't find it. I'll make sure I throw it at him next Christmas when he comes to the parade.

Back to how I became a king- Last year was the first time I had ever seen a parade and I couldn't help getting excited about it. My mister and his friends were the ones to build the actual float for the kings to ride on. They built it right in our backyard. It was very tall and brightly colored. It had three seats at the very top, one for each of the kings to sit on, kind of like a roost. Since my mister did such a good job, I decided to leave him a present right at the very top.

My plan was to lay the egg on the top seat and then hop off the float and find a place on the street to watch the parade. It took me a while to hop and fly all the way up there, but I finally arrived. Before I even got the chance to lay an egg, I heard a lot of people talking and saw my mister and his friends come out of the house and walk toward the float. He got on his tractor and started backing it up to the float. I'm not used to strangers, and I got a little nervous, so I hid behind a giant wire star. I sat there minding my own business as he pulled that float all the way to the start of the parade route. I tried not to make any noise while people climbed up onto the float and crowds gathered on the street below. To pass the time I laid my egg, then turned around and ate it since I was getting hungry.

My plan was to quietly ride until we got home again, then hop down and run to the coop, but that's not what happened. Once we started moving that giant wire star suddenly lit up so brightly it startled me and I started to squawk and fuss. That got the attention of one of the kings who was busy throwing candy at the children. When he noticed me, he started to laugh. He leaned over and picked me up. At first I thought he was going to throw me at the children, but instead he called me "Rey del Pollo" and lifted me high in the air so all the people below could see me. The crowd cheered and clapped, and suddenly, without even trying, I became the fourth Wise Man.

That was my one moment of glory, my flashing bit of fame. Once we got back home my mister carried me to the coop and I fell right to sleep. The next day I thought it was all a dream but when neighborhood folks kept coming by to look at me and congratulate my mister on his Rey del Pollo, I realized I realized I was famous.

I try not to let fame go to my head. I stay busy looking for candy to collect so I can use my beak to throw it to the children next year and I try to be the other thing all good kings should be- wise. Being wise is harder than it sounds, it means I have to learn to make good decisions. I think a wise chicken would not eat her own eggs, so I guess that's a start. Feliz Navidad until next year!

Joy to the World, Bethlehem, Judea 4 BC

T hings have been different around here since that baby was born. At first, I thought it was because we had never had a baby in our stable before, but now I think it's more than just that. It's hard to explain, I just feel happier. I feel content and peaceful. I feel like something very special has happened and I got to be here for it.

Of course, I've been around when other things have been born, and I'm a mother myself. But this was the first time a missus decided to have a baby in the stable. When she and her mister came in here, I thought they were lost. But they laid their blankets down on the ground like they were going to stay a while. I'm glad they had a lot of blankets, our stable is made of stone and it gets cold in here. That made me extra worried about the baby when he arrived. Speaking of that, it was hard on the the missus when she had her baby, she was in a lot of pain. I'm glad chickens lay eggs and not babies, I don't think I have a high tolerance for pain.

When the baby arrived, his mama wrapped him up in blankets and laid him in our manger. Our manger is a large rectangle of stone with a trough carved out on top. Usually it holds water, not babies. I was a little worried about the donkeys and the cows and the sheep because I didn't know where they would get water if they couldn't use the manger, water is life out here in the dry seasons. But somehow, that baby laying there where the water should be, seemed right.

That night we had some unexpected visitors. I had already gone to sleep, snuggled in a corner with my chicks sleeping under me, when a group of shepherds quietly tiptoed in to see the baby. At first, I didn't think it was proper for shepherds to be here, that baby was something special and shepherds were dirty and lowly regarded in our town. I've been out scratching around on the street in front of the stable and I've seen how the town people look down on shepherds. We have some people in our town who always dress in nice clothes. They're always very clean and when they go shopping, they have a servant with them to carry their things. I thought those fancy people should come and visit the baby, not shepherds. But then I remembered something I heard my mister say to his son once. He told him not to look down on shepherds because the greatest king Israel has ever had was King David, and he started out as a shepherd boy. So, once I thought of that, I looked a little more kindly at the shepherds who came to visit our baby. I was about to tuck my head into my wing and go back to sleep when the shepherds started to tell their story. Nothing could have made me go back to sleep after I heard that!

They said they had been out in the field watching over their sheep under the stars when suddenly, they saw a bright light and an angel standing before them. They said they were very afraid, and I didn't blame them for that. I've never seen an angel but it's always scary when something you don't expect and have never seen before surprises you. They said the angel told them,

Fear not! For behold, I bring you good tidings of great joy, which shall be to all people. For unto you is born this day in the City of David, a Savior, which is Christ the Lord. And this shall be a sign to you; you shall find the babe wrapped in swaddling clothes, lying in a manger.

And then, the sky was filled with angels and they all said together,

Glory to God in the highest, and on earth peace, good will toward men!

When the shepherds told us their story their faces shined- like they were angels themselves.

The baby and his parents stayed with us a while more. For all the time they were with us I tried to stay as close to them as I could, I didn't want me or my chicks to miss a single moment of what it was like to be with him. His parents called him Jesus and they said he would be the Savior of the world.

I've thought a lot about the word Savior and what it may mean. It's a word I had never heard before. The closest I can come to understanding it is like this- one time I was out on the edge of town scratching around near a patch of tall grass with my chicks when suddenly I saw an eagle swooping low and fast towards us. I immediately gave out my warning clucks and gathered my chicks under my wings for safety. A hen knows her chicks and I knew at once that one was missing. I clucked loudly and heard it chirp in return.

In a moment it rushed out of the tall grass and scooted under my wings, safe from harm. I think that's what a Savior does- protects their own. Sometimes I wonder what would have happened that day if the chick who had strayed away from me hadn't listened to my call. What if it was so busy chasing a cricket that it didn't hear my voice? All I know for sure is that I would never have left, I would have stayed forever, waiting for it to come back so I could love it and keep it safe. Somehow, I think the baby Jesus will be like that, except instead of just watching out for a small flock of chicks, he will be the Savior of the whole world.

As I fell asleep, I could feel my chicks breathing under my feathers, resting and dreaming of all they would do when they woke up in the morning. As I closed my eyes I thought of the shepherds. I thought of the light in their eyes when gave they their simple message- joy to the world, the Lord is born! I slept safe and warm that night- in the shadow of a baby, asleep in a manger.

By the Same Author

A Chicken Was There:

**Tales of the Pioneer Chickens Who
Helped Settle the Great American West**

From Jesse James to Buffalo Bill, from Westward Expansion to the Pony Express, the chickens who were eyewitnesses to history tell their stories in this collection of twenty-five short stories of the Great American West.

A Chicken Was There Too:

**Tales of the Colonial Chickens Who
Were There at the Birth of America**

From Benjamin Franklin to Paul Revere, from the Mayflower to Valley Forge, the chickens who were there at the birth of America tell their stories. Twenty-five short stories take the reader from the early explorers of America through the patriots of the Revolutionary War.

A Chicken Was There Also:

Tales of the Courageous Chickens Who Were There Through the Civil War and the Rebuilding of America

From the Underground Railroad to the Klondike Gold Rush, from the Statue of Liberty to the invention of the light bulb, the chickens who witnessed one of the most tumultuous times in American history tell their stories. Over the course of twenty-five short stories the history of America is told by the most unlikely of narrators.

About the Author

Arlene Davenport left a life of battling traffic in the big city for the life of watching the sunset in rural Texas. When she's not teaching junior high English, she spends her time reading, writing, gardening, and trying to survive the Texas heat. She lives in a small town south of Austin with her husband, two dogs, a cat, and fourteen chickens.

You can connect with Arlene on her Facebook author page: **A Chicken Was There**.

Made in United States
Troutdale, OR
11/27/2024